Plesiosaur

Hokuu

For Mom and Dad

EJ ALTBACKER

Enemy OF Oceans

raz**O**r
bill

An Imprint of Penguin Group (USA) Inc.

Shark Wars #5: Enemy of Oceans

RAZORBILL

Published by the Penguin Group

Penguin Young Readers Group

345 Hudson Street, New York, New York 10014, U.S.A.

Penguin Group (USA) Inc., 375 Hudson Street, New York, New York 10014, U.S.A.

Penguin Group (Canada), 90 Eglinton Avenue East, Suite 700, Toronto, Ontario, Canada M4P 2Y3 (a division of Pearson Penguin Canada Inc.)

Penguin Books Ltd, 80 Strand, London WC2R 0RL, England

Penguin Ireland, 25 St Stephen's Green, Dublin 2, Ireland (a division of Penguin Books Ltd)

Penguin Group (Australia), 250 Camberwell Road, Camberwell, Victoria 3124, Australia (a division of Pearson Australia Group Pty Ltd)

Penguin Books India Pvt Ltd, 11 Community Centre, Panchsheel Park, New Delhi – 110 017, India

Penguin Group (NZ), 67 Apollo Drive, Rosedale, Auckland 0632, New Zealand (a division of Pearson New Zealand Ltd)

Penguin Books (South Africa) (Pty) Ltd, 24 Sturdee Avenue, Rosebank, Johannesburg 2196, South Africa

Penguin Books Ltd, Registered Offices: 80 Strand, London WC2R 0RL, England

10 9 8 7 6 5 4 3 2 1

ISBN 978-1-59514-476-8

Library of Congress Cataloging-in-Publication Data is available

Printed in the United States of America

Enemy OF Oceans

CHAPTER 1

HOKUU STRUGGLED THROUGH THE TIGHT passage, forcing himself downward into the murky black of the Underwaters. Though he was built for tight spaces, like an eel, it had taken time and skill to wriggle this far. He had made his way into the seabed at a weak point in the eastern Sific fire waters after a series of seaquakes and volcanic eruptions.

Crossing between the two oceans was so dangerous that Hokuu, who as a frilled shark was used to the depths, was probably the only one in the Big Blue who could do it. Twice now he'd had to gather power from the waters with shar-kata, the ancient sharkkind martial art, to shield himself from being crushed.

Hokuu could tell he was close to the sealed-off ancient ocean because of the different taste of the water. Soon he could glimpse the glow of the lumos that provided the only light in the Underwaters. With one last push he was through, dislodging a few clumps of glowing coral that sank into the depths.

Hokuu marveled at the eerie world around him. The waters were warm, hot even, and seemed to glow, turning the darkness milky white. This small ocean— well, small for an ocean—had been sealed off for hundreds of thousands, maybe millions, of years. An enormous seaquake thirteen years ago had opened a slim passageway. That was when actual descendants of Tyro and First Shiver had found their way into the Big Blue for the first time in eons. They were living jurassic dwellers, prehistores that called themselves Fifth Shiver!

The sharkkind ruling the waters of the Big Blue above were a pale imitation of the glory that was— and the glory that should be once more! The pitiful modern sharkkind were shadows of their former selves; shadows of Fifth Shiver. Hokuu would help Fifth Shiver cross into the Big Blue and erase the weak sharkkind and dwellers that lived there. It was so simple.

But Bollagan, the former king of Fifth Shiver, had complicated matters. There was talk, talk, and more talk. He wanted to live in peace with the sharkkind above. He wanted to do nothing to the same sharks that had abused Hokuu's kind, the frilled sharks, since time unremembered.

No! That was unacceptable.

So Hokuu had organized a coup and put Drinnok in charge. Drinnok, like Hokuu, wanted to come up and conquer the Big Blue. But then came disaster. Hokuu's treacherous former apprentice closed the passage between the two oceans. However, this had given Hokuu time to think. His kind, the frilled sharks (or frills), hadn't changed like everyone else in the Big Blue. Frills were still glorious prehistores in both the Big Blue and the Underwaters! But today so few of them remained in the Big Blue.

Hokuu would not let their light wink out from the waters. The prehistores in the Underwaters would come up from the darkness and take their proper place in the ocean.

And Hokuu would be their king!

For that he needed Fifth Shiver and its new ruler, Drinnok. Hokuu scraped his tri-pointed teeth together as he sent ripples through his long body and propelled himself forward.

There weren't as many types of greenie in the Underwaters, but what did grow was gigantic. Some were carnivorous and had colorful flowers to attract prey, but most were bone white due to a lack of sunshine. He swam through the jagged spikes and spires where the white-greenie grew and into the Fifth Shiver homewaters, called Krator, the birthplace of Tyro and First Shiver. It was all sharp angles with an eerie, shadowless glow lighting up everything.

"Hold! Who dares swim in Fifth Shiver waters?" called a prehistore mako mariner. There were four more giants behind that one. Though Hokuu could have easily used his powers to send them to the Sparkle Blue for their disrespect, he could not have bested every sharkkind that lived in the Underwaters.

"I am Hokuu. Friend of King Drinnok and Fifth Shiver," he told them. "I wish to speak with your leader. He will want to see me."

The guards watched closely but led him into a clearing between two volcanic spires that glowed with a light as bright as a full moon because of the lumos attached to them. Hokuu was brought before Drinnok and his Line.

"I didn't think you would show your long and pointy face here again," the king growled. "Not after disappointing me for so long." Drinnok whipped his massive megalodon tail against a rock spire, splintering it to nothing.

As much as Hokuu hated admitting it, this was true. He had been stopped by his former apprentice who went by the absurd name Takiza Jaelynn Betta vam Delacrest Waveland ka Boom Boom, though Hokuu never gave him the satisfaction of calling him anything but Taki. It was Taki, a Siamese fighting betta fish, who had used his own shar-kata powers to close the first sea lane between the two oceans thirteen years ago. That was when Graynoldus's son Gray, now the Seazarein of the Big Blue, escaped from the Underwaters.

Then, not even a year ago, Hokuu had found another thin and treacherous passage to the Underwaters. This time he made sure that Gray and everyone else were preoccupied with other things, namely Finnivus and his Black Wave armada. It was Hokuu's unseen efforts that had caused all the strife in the waters then. He had woven that web like a sea spider. It was perfect.

Almost perfect.

Takiza had left Gray to deal with the threat of Finnivus on his own! Then the troublesome, preening betta fish had found Hokuu and destroyed his carefully laid plans again! Everything crumbled into the sand. And worse yet, Gray won his battle against Finnivus. He had grown into a leader and was named Seazarein of the Big Blue.

Both Takiza and Gray would have to be dealt with. Soon.

"Have you nothing to say? Did you come to the Underwaters to hover there like a fool?" asked the sneering Drinnok.

Hokuu dipped his snout and ignored the insult. "I live to serve you, King Drinnok. I know you're angry and I beg forgiveness." He would first prove himself to be loyal. After all, they both wanted the same thing: for Fifth Shiver to swim out from the Underwaters and take their rightful leadership position above everyone else in the Big Blue.

Well, almost the same thing.

Once the Big Blue was conquered, Hokuu would lead his kind, the frills, to victory. He would be the greatest ruler the oceans had ever seen. But he wouldn't breathe a word of this to Drinnok.

"It was our enemies above who kept you from returning to the wider waters. I am working every moment so that the sons and daughters of Tyro will once again swim free!"

"Empty words will not get us out of here," Drinnok replied. "Or earn you a place on my Line, if that is still your goal."

"It is! It is!" Hokuu said. "But I would help you anyway because it's the right thing to do."

"Enough of this! Do you have a way out or don't you? The earth above and below us buckles and heaves. One day—perhaps soon—the Underwaters will cease to exist. Everyone here will be turned into paste when the rock above our heads smashes to the ground beneath us."

Hokuu nodded. "It will take me a week, but I can create a passageway for you and your mariners. After that, you can take revenge on those who have struggled to keep you imprisoned here by closing the passage between the Underwaters and the Big Blue."

Drinnok scraped his huge dagger teeth together. "That I will. We all will."

A rumbling laugh echoed in the pale half-light and Grimkahn—a mosasaur, the largest type of jurassic dweller—glided into the clearing. "You promise this overgrown worm a spot in your Line? There must be a mistake, Drinnok. I speak for the jurassics and I'm mightier than any frill. A spot on the Line is my due in the new world of the Big Blue!"

Hokuu held his tongue. It wasn't his place to argue in King Drinnok's court. Besides, Grimkahn's species was the strongest of the jurassic dwellers. Even with Hokuu's powers, it wouldn't be a sure thing to win a battle against him. Grimkahn was eighty feet long and had giant, clawed flippers and a gaping sea crocodile's mouth that could swallow a twenty-foot shark whole. Well, if not whole, it wouldn't take him more than a few bites.

Grimkahn would make a powerful ally if he could be turned, thought Hokuu.

In the Big Blue, sharkkind were the undisputed leaders of the oceans. The dwellers there, while many more in number than sharkkind, could never muster a force that would threaten a strong shiver of sharks. But in the Underwaters that wasn't necessarily true. The dwellers here, such as giant turtles, or even crabs, were immense. And larger still were a subset of the dwellers called the jurassics. These were marine reptiles such as plesiosaurs, pliosaurs, and many others. While all were considered dwellers, the enormous jurassics ruled them all. And the mosasaurs were the strongest of the giants.

"You speak for the dwellers, that is true," Drinnok told the mosasaur. "But you are dwellers, not sharkkind. Fifth Shiver rules sharkkind and dwellers, including you jurassics. The Five in the Line have always been sharkkind and Hokuu is a shark, even though he's a frill, so he can be considered. That's the way it's been since the time of Tyro."

No one noticed Hokuu's grimace at the insult. Most sharkkind looked alike: with a dorsal fin on the back and a divided tail. Not frilled sharks. They were cousins with the eels and shared their sinewy form, which Hokuu thought was pleasing and sleek. Other sharks mistrusted them for it, though.

Regular sharkkind were afraid of them. Called them monsters. They would suffer.

Grimkahn roared in frustration so loudly that it was both painful and terrible to hear. "Tyro is gone! In the new world above, there should be new ways. The jurassics demand their due!"

"Keep a civil tongue in my homewaters, Grimkahn, or you will lose it!" Drinnok snarled.

A smaller jurassic, a plesiosaur, whipped its slender neck back and forth. "He's disrespecting you, leader! I invoke the right of challenge!"

There was dead silence in the clearing. Hokuu heard one of the carnivorous bladders in the white-greenie shut with a snap as it ate something smaller and weaker.

This would be interesting.

Drinnok ignored the plesiosaur and stared at Grimkahn. "If you can't discipline this long-necked fool, there will be consequences."

Grimkahn smiled his immense crocodile smile. "Unlike you, I don't control every word from my subjects' mouths. I allow them their own judgment. It so happens that Breaker's judgment is that you're unfit to rule."

"It is!" agreed Breaker. "You're an old fool, Drinnok. Fight me if you dare!"

Grimkahn swung his huge head around and hit Breaker in the side with his giant snout. "Now, now, Breaker. You're being rude. I won't order you to apologize, but you should."

"I won't!" Breaker said.

Grimkahn shook his head apologetically. "I guess you'll have to ignore the insult, Drinnok. Or teach him manners . . . if you dare."

The rest of Drinnok's Line looked at their king. There was no way he could back down from the challenge. Grimkahn was much smarter than Hokuu had given him credit for. Drinnok swam off the Speakers Rock. "You desire single combat? So be it!"

9

Breaker was a large plesiosaur, fast and young, but Drinnok was a fully grown megalodon. Though the king was smaller from snout to tail, the megalodon's toothy mouth was much bigger. It was youth against experience, strength versus speed.

Drinnok swam straight at Breaker, who darted off to the side. He twisted his supple neck around lightning fast and scored a bite into the megalodon's flank. Breaker was after him again, in a flash, going for Drinnok's tail. But the leader of Fifth Shiver had swum in a thousand battles before this one. He created space by cutting a turn around a rock spire and threw himself into a spinning turn. Now, instead of chasing Drinnok's tail, Breaker was facing his toothy maw. The plesiosaur tried to slow himself but Drinnok ripped off his front left flipper. Blood streamed from the wound.

"No!" screamed Breaker. "You weren't supposed to do that! Help me, Grimkahn! Help!"

Drinnok turned to the mosasaur. "It seems this pup wants you to take him home. Do you wish me to spare his pathetic life?"

Grimkahn ignored Breaker's cries. "As you said, you lead Fifth Shiver, which rules the dwellers. It's your choice whether to show mercy."

"Yes, oh great king!" cried Breaker. "Mercy! I think this may heal. We jurassics can sometimes swim with only three flippers!"

Drinnok snapped his giant jaws down on Breaker's slender neck, chopping his head off and ending his pleading.

The megalodon looked at Grimkahn, who was expressionless. "It was Breaker's choice to defy me, much like the sharkkind above. For that, Breaker's life—and theirs above—are forfeits." Drinnok waved a fin at the plesiosaur's body. "Besides, the crabs I rule also need to eat, Grimkahn. Remember that."

Drinnok and his Five in the Line laughed as the giant mosasaur and his jurassics swam away.

Hokuu was glad he had made the trip. All this time he had wondered how to gain the upper fin over Drinnok while exalting his own kind, the frills, so they could exalt him in turn. The answer had been in the Underwaters all this time.

Grimkahn and his jurassics were the force that Hokuu needed to make sure that Drinnok did everything he wanted once the Big Blue was conquered.

11

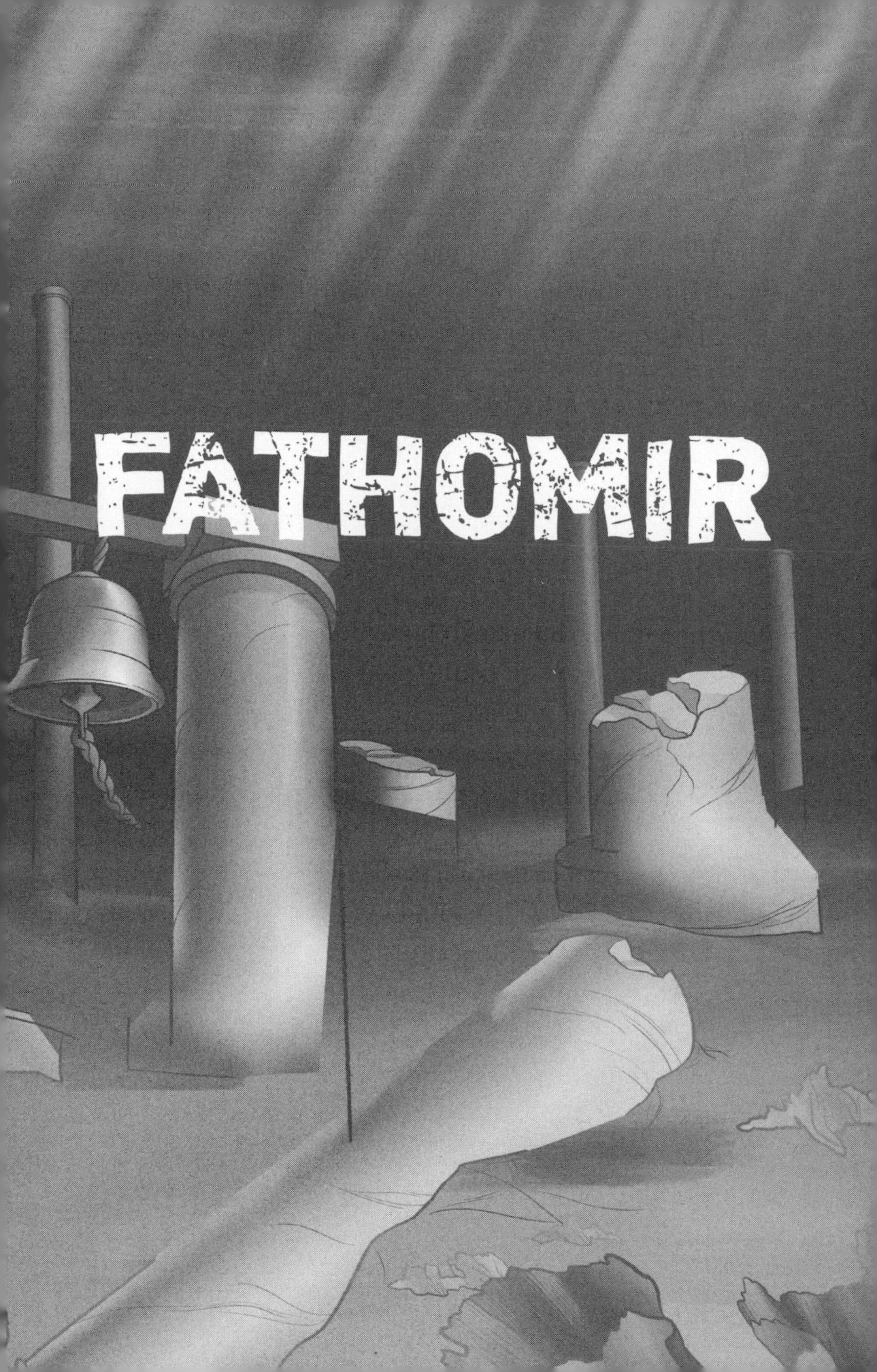
FATHOMIR

CHAPTER 2

GRAY RESTED HIS POWERFUL PECTORAL FINS
on the Seazarein's throne as he waited for the sharkkind and dwellers in front of him to get organized. He
had been impressed when he saw the previous Seazarein, Kaleth, using the throne the first time he swam
into the golden greenie of the Fathomir homewaters.
At the time, Gray had only been the leader of Riptide Shiver and didn't want even that responsibility.
Though it had only been a few months since then, so
much had happened it seemed like ages ago.

Oh, to only be the leader of Riptide, Gray thought.
That would be sweet.

The problems Gray faced were much smaller
then. He became Seazarein after Kaleth was sent to
the Sparkle Blue by Hokuu, the evil frill shark. As
Seazarein, Gray could feel the weight of the mountain
above pressing down on him. He discovered that

resting his fins on the Seazarein's throne was a terrible duty.

Decisions large and small were his—and his alone—to make.

And so were the costs.

The throne did provide a great view of everyone in the cavern, which was lit by colorful anemones and urchins that shined brightly so everyone could see. Today, several quickfins had arrived from distant corners of the Big Blue. Quickfins were fast dwellers and sharkkind that carried messages and information between the ancient shivers.

In Gray's short time as Seazarein, he had grown to dislike whenever one of these messengers came to Fathomir. It seemed every single quickfin brought a new and unexpected problem that needed his immediate attention. And that distracted Gray from his biggest problem—finding Hokuu. The frill wanted nothing more than to plunge the Big Blue into chaos and make the oceans flow red with blood.

And I have no idea where he is, thought Gray as he ground his teeth.

"Silence!" yelled Judijoan by his left side. The long and skinny oarfish hovered straight up and down, towering over everyone else. She glared through the red spines of her dorsal fin, which grew out of her forehead, giving the old teacher a stern dignity. "Swim forward one at a time in the order that you arrived. After your message has been delivered, leave the cavern and wait outside as there may be a return message. No one else should be speaking but the quickfin ordered to do so. So the rest of you, be quiet!"

Barkley, hovering to Gray's right, whispered, "And we thought Miss Lamprey was bad." Miss Lamprey had been their teacher when they were growing up in the Caribbi Sea. Judijoan had been Kaleth's advisor and knew everything about protocol and history, so Gray kept her in that position. He had also made Barkley an advisor, much to Judijoan's shock, as he was to her only a dogfish. But Barkley was Gray's oldest and best friend. Plus, he was smart and many times saw things that no one else did.

The first quickfin, a wahoo shaped like a silvery urchin spine, came forward so only Gray, Barkley, and Judijoan could hear. "I come with greetings from Minister Prime of Indi Shiver, Tydal. Code word: Starfish."

With any true quickfin message, there was always a code word known only to the Seazarein's advisors. This month the code words all began with the letter S.

"Minister Prime?" Gray asked, as he had never heard of the title before.

"He did not want to take the title of king, and since there was already a mariner prime leading the armada he decided to call himself Minister Prime."

"I see. And what does the minister prime say?"

"Only that things are going well and he wishes you a long reign in your new role as Seazarein." The wahoo dipped his snout and left.

Indi Shiver used to be led by a madfish named Finnivus who wanted to conquer the entire Big Blue. Gray had to swim out and lead Riptide United, consisting of AuzyAuzy, Hammer, Vortex, and many other shivers, along with the orcas, and with them had finally defeated Finnivus and his Black Wave armada. After they were defeated Gray had tried to appoint a shark from a ruling family of Indi but every time he did, all the other ruling families had objected.

Finally, in absolute exasperation, Gray chose the First Court Shark. The princes and princesses said yes, thinking they would assassinate the poor fin later after they were done bickering among themselves. But Gray liked the idea of a non-royal leading so he didn't let that happen. He left five hundred mariners under the command of Xander del Hav'aii—third in the AuzyAuzy Line—to keep the peace and protect Tydal. He also didn't let the princes and princesses return, keeping them as his guests.

Barkley gave Gray a thoughtful look. "It seems the currents are joyfully smooth at Indi Shiver." Gray could tell that his friend didn't believe this. Neither did he, for another Indi messenger was waiting.

"I come from Indi Shiver with a message from Xander del Hav'aii," this quickfin told them.

"Oh boy," Gray let slip. Judijoan gave him a critical shake of her long tail. Seazarein were not supposed to say things like *oh boy* for everyone to hear.

"The message is as follows. 'There have been two attempts on Tydal's life, the last by a squaline. I am useless here. Request to be sent back to AuzyAuzy homewaters.' That is the end of the message. Code word: Starfish."

Judijoan waved her tail to make the next quickfin wait as the last left the cavern. She swam closer to Gray so no one else would hear. "If Tydal was attacked by his personal guard then one of the royal families is behind it."

"Probably more than one," Barkley added. "And Xander doesn't seem too happy."

Gray nodded. The squaline were the personal guard to the throne and supposed to be above the petty power plays between the royal families. For one of them to betray this duty was unheard of. If Tydal was killed, there would most likely be a civil war in the Indi Ocean between the royal families.

Just what I need, Gray thought.

Judijoan waved the next quickfin messenger over when Gray nodded. This one was a swordfish and dipped her bill to Gray. "I come from AuzyAuzy Shiver, sent by Eyes and Ears Leilani. Code word: Sunfish."

"Code's right, but what's 'eyes and ears'?" Barkley asked Judijoan.

"They are information gatherers. They are known as spyfish, although most of them don't go skulking about," Judijoan answered. "Leilani is one of the youngest ever to attain the rank of Eyes and Ears, from what I understand. They listen to reports from around the ocean to uncover plots and intrigue. Most ancient shivers have them."

"How come I've never heard of these Eyes and Ears spyfish?" asked Barkley. "Are they like ghostfins?" Ghostfins were a small force of super scouts created by Barkley. These were fish that could swim unseen inside an enemy's camp.

"They wouldn't be very good spyfish if everyone knew of them, now would they?" Judijoan answered. "But no, they try to see the big picture. They are thinkers."

Gray flicked a fin for the swordfish to continue.

"One patrol is missing in the fire waters. Another was driven away by a freak whorl current before it could finish its patrol. That is all." The swordfish left.

"I don't get that message," Barkley said. "The fire waters are a dangerous place. Things like that happen. Why tell us at all if there's no point?"

Judijoan sent a ripple through her long oarfish body, calling the next messenger. "Sometimes information is sent with no conclusion because it seems odd and you might notice a pattern. But most of the time nothing is exactly that. Nothing."

The last fish waiting moved forward. It was a four-winged flying fish. Apparently, these fish could leap from the water and glide above the ocean using their long tails to force themselves into the air time and time again, literally skipping across the surface. Some could stay out of the water for half a mile!

This young flying fish flicked its upper and lower fins, angling them downward in a smart salute that displayed their blue highlights nicely. "Quickfin Speedmeister with a message from Grinder, leader of Hammer Shiver. Code word: Seaweed. The message is as follows—"

"Hold it, hold it," Barkley said, waving his tail for the messenger to stop. "Your name is Speedmeister?"

"Well, that's what it should be, 'cause I'm so fast. Faster than a wahoo, even," the flying fish answered. "My real name is Eugene, though, your lordships."

Gray laughed along with Barkley. Judijoan scowled. "What is your message, Eugene?"

Eugene did another smart salute, flicking his four fin wings down and up. "The message is as follows. 'Hope everything is going well, friend and battle brother Gray. Would love to see you and everyone else at the Tuna Run. I'll be there with Hammer Shiver and we will be catching the most bluefin because we are, of course, the best.' End of message."

Gray and Barkley laughed some more. Grinder's personality really came through in the message.

"Oh, I'd love to go," Barkley said with a grin. The Tuna Run was where big, fat bluefin whipped across the undersea mountain range called the Atlantis Spine. Many shivers would be there, and it was a fine place to stuff yourself on the most delicious fish in the sea.

"Wouldn't that be great?" Gray remarked. "But there's no way."

Judijoan shook her head, causing the red plume overhanging her head to move back and forth briskly. "That is correct, Graynoldus. Only after you solve all the ocean's problems can you waste your time at the Tuna Run."

"I thought the Seazarein could do whatever he wanted," Barkley said, teasing.

"That's true," Judijoan answered with another scowl. "As long as he maintains the schedule I set for him. And on my schedule there's no time for foolishness."

"She's right, Bark," Gray agreed. He noticed that the flying fish was still there. "Speedmeister? Is there something else?"

"Yes," the flying fish said. "I carry a second message. Code word: Blue Coral."

"That's an old code," Judijoan said.

"From the North Atlantis, near Riptide Shiver, which doesn't exist anymore," added Barkley.

Hokuu had been responsible for that also, and

that brought the frilled shark back into Gray's mind. Where was he? They would have to find him. They couldn't leave him to do whatever he was planning, that was for sure.

The quickfin bobbed his snout. "Yes, that's true. Which is why I didn't want to give the message, but the code word was good so maybe it's just old. But also, a stonefish gave this message to me."

"A stonefish?" Judijoan gasped. "Kaleth didn't know any of those poisonous criminals."

"Yeah, but we do," Gray said as Barkley gave him a look. "It has to be Trank. What's the message, Speedmeister?"

"Don't call him that," Judijoan said. "You'll only encourage him."

Barkley nodded for Eugene to continue.

"The message is as follows. 'From Trank, the owner and operator of Slaggernacks, home of the Big Blue's tastiest seasoned fish, comes a new experience, the Stingeroo Supper Club, now open for business and conveniently located outside the Fathomir homewaters. Come for the fish; stay for the good times. All Seazareins eat free.' End of message. Nice to meet you, your lordships." Eugene flitted out of the cavern in a flash.

"What does that mean?" asked the confused Judijoan.

"With Trank you never know," Barkley told her

with a frown. The stonefish had his fins in many dark and mysterious things.

"If he's inviting us over, there's a definite reason." Gray said. "We need to go. Besides, couldn't you go for some seasoned fish?"

Barkley grumbled and shook his head.

CHAPTER 3

VELENKA PROWLED THE GOLD-GREENIE OF THE
Fathomir homewaters. Her black hide would normally
be an advantage for concealing herself, but today was
bright and sunny. Thankfully, the towering kelp field
went on for miles, so Velenka could remain hidden if
she swam with caution. She needed to be both silent
and focused to catch something to eat. But her unwanted companion was neither of those things, which
made hunting difficult.

"It's so beautiful here," Mari said.

"Would you please be quiet?" Velenka hissed.
"Some of us are trying to find lunch."

"It kind of reminds me of the Riptide homewaters."
The thresher sniffled.

"Other than the fact they look nothing alike?"
Velenka said. "Now, shhh!"

The Riptide homewaters had been destroyed
by Hokuu. Velenka had been used as a decoy in the

frilled shark's intricate plan, which ended when he sent Gray's predecessor Kaleth and most of her finja guardians to the Sparkle Blue. Right now, Velenka was technically still a prisoner and so guarded at all times. More often than not, Mari was given this duty. The thresher didn't have anything to worry about, though. Velenka wasn't about to escape.

She had nowhere to go.

For weeks now Velenka had to listen to everyone's sad stories of where they were when Kaleth was killed, or this friend, or that one, or what they'd been doing when Riptide was destroyed. None of those things bothered her. No, what bothered Velenka was that she had been used as a part of Hokuu's plan and hadn't figured that out until it was far too late.

Velenka had a mind that could see the layers of action needed to get her to a seemingly impossible goal. She was smart. At least that was what her teachers had said when she was younger. They had filled her full of knowledge of tactics and deception, tricks and ploys, and all manner of ruses. But Hokuu had played on her vanities and Velenka swam along like a jelly-headed fool. Not that Gray, Barkley, or any of the rest believed her. They thought she was somehow turning a plot within a plot.

If only . . .

I was used like a stupid pup! she yelled inside her mind.

How she would love to revenge herself on Hokuu. But she feared the frill. He was too strong. There was no way she could get back at him. That was the worst part. Velenka was helpless when it came to him and she hated that.

Mari sniffled again. She was a harmless shark who had even shown kindness to Velenka on a few occasions. Since the destruction of Riptide, where she'd watched hundreds of mariners be roasted alive by Hokuu's deadly shar-kata powers, Mari hadn't been the same. The thresher couldn't forget. Velenka had noticed this same thing in mariners who had fought too many battles. Even if they escaped with no visible injuries, they were damaged. It was as if they were scarred on the inside by their experiences. But in the Big Blue, every day was a day when you could have lunch, or be lunch. Velenka couldn't allow herself to be infected by Mari's weakness.

Especially when Hokuu was still out there.

"Are you going to start crying again?" she asked the thresher. "Don't. It scares the fish."

Mari swam off a little ways. Velenka glided forward, following a haddock as it hunted shrimp. It would be the distracted haddock's last mistake. She moved forward, gaining speed, and then struck. Victory! She gnashed her teeth together, enjoying the fish as she drifted between the stalks of golden greenie.

Mari came over, shaking her head. "I don't see

how you can stuff yourself like it's the Tuna Run after all that's happened."

"It's not a matter of sympathy, which is useless," Velenka told her. "It's a matter of you not being able to leave the past in your wake."

"Unbelievable! Do you have any feelings at all?"

"Shhh!" Velenka hissed. "What was that?"

Mari listened for a moment. "It's just the water pushing the greenie."

"No, I heard something over there." Velenka gestured with a fin. "Something big. Let's swim back to the throne cavern."

"You heard nothing and I'll prove it," the thresher said.

Velenka bumped Mari before she could go too far. "Don't be stupid," she whispered. She knew something was lurking. "The ocean is a dangerous place."

Mari went forward anyway. She didn't take two tail strokes before a mako finja materialized and rushed toward her. It was one of the renegades!

Mari was unprepared for the attack, but the mako roared past her—and straight at Velenka!

Velenka cut a sharp turn and used a giant kelp formation as an obstacle so the shark couldn't strike her tail as Mari watched. "Help me!" Velenka yelled at the other shark.

But Mari was paralyzed with fear, her long-lobed tail flicking but not moving her body through the water. A second mako appeared, accelerating to attack speed toward her, and still Mari did nothing. She waited for death.

Velenka had no time to help the thresher, as if she'd ever do something so stupid. She cut and dodged, passing by Mari while evading her pursuer.

The mako formed a two-shark formation: switching places and weaving through the water with deadly grace. Just as both Velenka and Mari were about to become chowder, a few stalks of ropy kelp shot upward, blocking their attackers. The makos were going too fast to stop and swam right into the gold-greenie. It fouled their tail strokes for a moment.

"Swim for your life!" Velenka yelled to Mari.

It took the mako only a few seconds to get free and close the distance to strike. Velenka was sure they wouldn't get lucky again, so she faced the renegades. If she was to swim the Sparkle Blue today, she would go down fighting.

But suddenly Takiza was there. The tiny betta fish zipped out of nowhere and snapped one of his colorful, gauzy fins into the lead shark's side. Though the force of a tail flick by a dweller so small shouldn't have done anything, the mako was blasted into its partner and both ended up a hundred feet away.

"You were lucky today, Velenka," the larger mako growled. "You're a traitor and Hokuu always keeps his promises about sending traitors to the Sparkle Blue."

Takiza hovered in the warm current, his fins billowing majestically. "You are mistaken," the Siamese fighting fish announced. "Hokuu never keeps his promises. If he's made one to you, I would advise you to grow eyes on your tail so you may watch it."

The second mako spat and ground his needle teeth together. "He'll deal with you, too, Takiza! You'll see!"

"Hokuu knows where to find me," the betta replied. "Now swim along to your master. Or do you prefer to try your clumsy attack against me once more?"

The makos glowered but left, fading into the waters.

A familiar voice asked, "Are they gone?"

Velenka and Mari looked down, surprised to see Snork swimming to them from the seabed.

The sawfish wagged his long bill. "I wanted to help but wasn't fast enough, so I cut through some greenie as a distraction. Did it help?"

So that was how the greenie entangled the charging makos. Velenka was impressed despite herself.

"You saved us, Snork," Mari told him. "I mean, until Takiza saved us."

The betta swam around Snork, eyeing his bill. "Tell me, Snork, is it? That kelp was almost as thick as Velenka's body—"

"Hey, that's not fair!" exclaimed Velenka, insulted. "I was locked up and couldn't exercise for a long time!"

Takiza continued speaking to Snork. "Have you cut through many things that thick before?"

"When I was little, I used to all the time," Snork answered. "Dad and I would go out and do all sorts of fun stuff, games where we would race to see who could cut things into shapes, or into the most pieces. But then Mom found out and stopped it. She said using my bill like that would make me go blind."

The betta snorted. "Amusing. But . . . the greenie moved upward faster than if it had merely floated."

"I pushed it," Snork said proudly as he showed them the motion of forcing his bill upward. "Dad taught me that, too. The trick is to concentrate real hard. I had to try and help Mari."

"And me," Velenka said. "You wanted to save me, too? Right?"

Takiza shooed the mako away with a frilly fin. "Tell me, Snork, have you ever heard the term *bladefish*?"

"I don't think so," the sawfish answered, waving his bill back and forth.

"Interesting. We will speak later." Takiza turned to Mari. "Now, I must ask, what were you doing?"

The thresher sputtered, "Um, Velenka was hungry and—"

The betta slashed his fins through the water, silencing her. "What were you doing swimming out so foolishly after Velenka told you she thought there was danger?"

"See?" Velenka said.

"I—I—didn't think—"

"No, you did not," Takiza told Mari. "It was pure chance I was swimming nearby and overheard. A wise fish is always wary, even when there seems to be no danger at all."

"I suppose you're right," Mari replied, chastened. "I'm sorry."

Takiza softened and swam closer to the thresher. He brushed her forehead with his small fin. "The best thing you can do for the friends you have lost is to not join them," he told her.

Then the betta gestured everyone toward Fathomir and they went.

Velenka doubted that the Siamese fighting fish just happened to be close enough to hear their conversation. She was being watched. She didn't like that fact but it had saved her life today. The more unsettling news was that Hokuu still wanted her gone from the Big Blue. Not only couldn't she get even with Hokuu, she was still the frilled shark's prey.

What could Velenka possibly do about that?

She had absolutely no idea.

CHAPTER 4

"WOW!" EXCLAIMED GRAY WHEN THEY GOT nearer the Stingeroo Supper Club and could hear a group of dolphins singing in their native tongue, click-razz. "Who knew this was here?"

The place was hidden inside a forest of dense greenie a mile outside of Fathomir's territory and couldn't be seen at all from the outside.

"I did," Shear told Gray and Barkley. "We know everything that goes on around the homewaters." Shear, a prehistore tiger shark, was the leader of the Seazarein's finja guardians at Fathomir. Back when Gray was named Aquasidor, Shear had been the captain of his guard. Since there currently was no Aquasidor, the big tiger now used his depleted finja force to protect Gray wherever he went.

"Does everything include Hokuu's finja makos almost killing Mari and Velenka?" Barkley asked.

Gray gave his friend a bump. It was hard to patrol an area as big as Fathomir with the few specially trained mariners Shear had left. They did need to tighten security, though. Shear had taken Kaleth's loss personally and held himself responsible even though the blame for everything could be put squarely on Hokuu.

"No one blames you for that," Gray told the big tiger. "Have you talked with Striiker?" Striiker was a longtime friend of Gray and Barkley's, and led Riptide Shiver now that Gray was Seazarein.

"Yes," Shear answered. "I'm going to have him begin patrols with the Riptide mariners he has available who are not protecting your shiver sharks. Though their training isn't up to guardian standards, I suppose they could be helpful."

Barkley bristled at this comment. "At least Riptide is helping while they're settling in," he said, eyeing Shear. "That's nice of them, don't you think?"

Gray gave Barkley another bump to remind him not to push the guardian tiger shark too far. Since the destruction of their homewaters, Riptide had been homeless. Gray wouldn't allow his family and friends to wander the ocean like jelly drifters, so as Seazarein, he gave them a chunk of territory and a swath of the golden greenie as their hunting grounds. Shear hadn't liked that decision because of the security risk but Gray wouldn't budge.

The group swam through the thick greenie curtain toward the music. Inside this barrier was a large area where most of the kelp and seaweed had been cleared. What was left seemed to be there for decoration. Lumos were plastered everywhere. Since the sun was shining straight down this time of day, their light wasn't noticeable, but at night it would be beautiful.

Sharkkind, none of whom Gray recognized, hovered in clumps of twos, threes, and fours as they ate seasoned fish prepared by skilled shellhead dwellers who stuffed them with tasty greenie and mosses from around the watery world. This environment was different from Slaggernacks but just as fun. This was exactly what Gray needed. A little time to clear his head and relax!

"I see too many lionfish swimming about for it to be natural," Shear commented. "They are usually loners."

Barkley gave Gray a look, agreeing with the tiger. "And those are just the ones you can see. Oh, you'll love this place, Shear. It's delightfully full of poisonous dwellers. Trank hires them out to be assassins from time to time."

"What?" The tiger turned to Gray. "Then this place is too dangerous for you to be here. We should leave and I'll order my mariners to attack before nightfall."

Gray spied a group of rocks and reached out with his senses. Sure enough, he could tell that many of the rocks weren't rocks at all, but stonefish. He had a feeling one of them was Trank and decided to have a little fun. "So, you think you could wipe this place out in the next day or two?"

"I wouldn't need that long," the finja captain answered. "I didn't realize this was a nest of killers, or I would have already done it."

"Well, since I don't see any friendly faces, or free orders of seasoned fish . . ."

"Whoa, whoa, sharkkind," Trank said as he stopped acting like a rock and swam up from the pile Gray had been watching. "Is that any way for youse to treat an old friend? Especially when I have your favorite south seas flavored bluefin with volcano sauce being made as we speak? And it's never been proven that anyone died of anything other than natural causes where I was concerned."

Shear had chomped his teeth in surprise at stonefish's sudden appearance. Barkley couldn't be happier at his startled reaction and rubbed it in.

"Look at that. Gray and I, the two poorly trained Riptide Shiver mariners, didn't flinch at all because of Trank but you did. Maybe you could use a little training tune up."

Shear glared at the dogfish.

"Quit bumping snouts you two," Gray told the pair. He turned to the stonefish and said, "I was only kidding, Trank. How's Gafin doing?"

Gafin was the reputed king of the urchins who controlled all criminal activity in the North Atlantis. Supposedly, Trank worked for him, but Gray and Barkley didn't know for sure. Trank was something of a mystery. There had been times when he helped Gray and his friends in the war against Finnivus. But another time it seemed Trank had betrayed them. The stonefish always came up with a great explanation for why he did whatever he did, though.

"He's good," Trank answered. "He sends regards and congratulations, but also his regrets at not being able to be here today. Follow me, please." The stonefish's tiny fins circled as he led them deeper into Stingeroo. "I've been saving the best spot in the place for youse. And don't worry, it's private."

The stonefish took them to an area in a maze of coral that formed a cavern over their heads. You could see and hear the musical group through a number of honeycombed openings that also allowed a nice current to flow.

But there was only one way in or out unless you were Trank's size.

"I don't like it. This isn't safe," Shear told Gray.

Trank turned and faced the giant tiger shark. "Not safe? Sharkkind, youse is safer here than under your momma's belly when youse was a pup." He gestured with his fins to the opening they had swum through. Now there were long strands of clear greenie hanging in front of the opening. Then Gray realized it wasn't greenie at all. They were jellyfish tentacles! A swarm was tumbling with the light current and blocking the opening. Not only that, they were the most dangerous jellies in the Big Blue.

"Box jellyfish!" Barkley gasped as he watched the translucent, square jellyfish.

"That's right, dogfish," Trank said, nodding with pride. "And nobody, but nobody, swims through a swarm of box jellies."

"This is crazy," Shear grunted. "Dwellers and jellies do not work together."

"Most dwellers, and all sharkkind, do not work or talk to jellies. But I and my new jelly friends share a certain, how can I put it—"

"Poisonous-ness?" Barkley offered.

Trank shrugged. "Youse isn't far off the mark, doggie. We venomous dwellers are mistrusted by youse regular types in the Big Blue, misguided as everyone is about our gentle and honest natures."

Gray gave Barkley a tail slap before he could throw out a smart comment.

Trank went on, "It turns out the less poisonous jellies don't like the more poisonous ones, either. So, out of the goodness of our hearts, we bonded with these friendless dwellers and formed an arrangement profitable to both of us."

"What could they possibly need from you?" asked Shear.

"That youse don't need to know," Trank answered.

Shear ground his teeth. "You cannot stay in here forever, stonefish. And you will tell me how you were able to get a quickfin code word."

Trank flicked his tail at Shear. "Whoa, whoa! Please, stop. For your own sake. It just so happens that making threats to me in my own place happens to be very, very bad luck, Shear-the-guardian-captain-of-the-finja-at-Fathomir. Fins who do that tend to have shockingly horrible, bloody accidents soon after making those threats."

"Why, you—"

Gray bumped Shear away from Trank. "How about nobody threatens anyone today?" he said. "I'm here for a nice meal and to hear some music. I don't want to spend my limited free time having to yell at anyone for acting like a chowderheaded moron. Is that understood?"

"Got it! Sorry," Trank said. "I apologize to everyone." Shear also nodded.

"I do have a question for you," Gray went on. "And I'm asking this as the Seazarein and a friend."

"Since youse added that last part, ask away," the stonefish replied.

"Why are you here?"

Trank opened and closed his mouth a few times, thinking before he answered. "I'm here because you're here."

"What does that mean?" Barkley asked suspiciously.

"Not like that," the stonefish said. "Youse see, the people I work with, the leaders of the families in the other oceans, their business sunk to nothing when that psycho Finnivus was around. And youse solved that problem, permanent-like. And since Gray and I worked together in the Atlantis . . ."

"So, you're here to help Gray?" Barkley asked. "Seriously?"

"Very seriously," Trank told them. "Profits have never been better than during this peace youse created. Gafin and the other urchin kings want it to stay that way. Nice and quiet."

"Could you tell me where Hokuu is?" asked Gray. "That would help."

Trank shook his head. "I'm glad youse asked about him because he concerns the urchin kings. Maybe it's better for everyone if youse take him out like with Finnivus?"

Shear slashed his tail through the water but kept his temper. "The Seazarein is not a contract killer, stonefish."

"Not saying he is, though I think Gray would be pretty great at it if he tried," Trank said. "That's a compliment. As it is, we don't know exactly where Hokuu is, but we think the fire waters in the South Sific are a good place for youse to check."

"And why do you think that?" asked Barkley.

"Because everyone I send there doesn't come back," Trank told them.

Everyone was silent, considering.

"Your meal will arrive shortly. Enjoy yourselves and don't forget to tell your friends about the Stingeroo Supper Club." The stonefish swam out one of the openings in the wall to the main area.

"As if that means anything," Shear commented after Trank left.

Barkley sighed. "Unfortunately, it kind of does."

Gray nodded. "It looks like we need to go visit Kendra and AuzyAuzy Shiver and speak with this Eyes and Ears shark, Leilani. Something is going on in the fire waters and we need to find out what."

INDI SHIVER

CHAPTER 5

TYDAL GAZED ACROSS THE FLOATING GREENIE Gardens of Indi, trying to order his troubled thoughts. The gardens were famous as one of the true wonders of the Big Blue. It was a collection of the most beautiful kelp, coral, seaweed, and sea flowers in all the seven seas tended by master dwellers who trimmed and pruned them to perfection. Walls of delicate coral moved back and forth allowing the blooms to be caught by the current and whisked upward to create swimming lanes of dazzling color both above and below.

Besides the skilled shellheads and fins who took care of the gardens, no one but royalty had been allowed to look at this marvel for ages. Finnivus, the former leader of Indi, hadn't even let other royals see the gardens, preferring to keep them for his own enjoyment. Tydal wanted to open the marvel to everyone, but they were located near his royal quarters and there had been two attempts on his life already so he couldn't for safety reasons.

His safety.

All this beauty and no one to enjoy it, Tydal thought. Not even me.

At least Finnivus could take pleasure in the fabulous gardens because he didn't care about anyone but himself. It added to his enjoyment that others wanted to see them and couldn't. Tydal shook his head, remembering.

Finnivus was the reason for Indi Shiver's fall. The vain fool had declared war on the entire Big Blue. He didn't stop until the Indi armada was crushed and he was sent to the Sparkle Blue in the titanic Battle of the Maw in the Atlantis. Tydal didn't miss or mourn the former emperor. As First Court Fish, he had lived in fear of being sentenced to death every day of his life. No, Tydal was glad Finnivus was gone.

The victorious force in that fight, Riptide United, had been led by Gray. Tydal thought him a bold and cunning leader. It was Gray—now the Seazarein of the entire Big Blue!—who had imposed the sanctions on Indi Shiver after their loss. The Black Wave armada was disbanded, their mariner force made smaller, and five hundred AuzyAuzy sharkkind were left in the Indi homewaters to watch them. This was actually better than Tydal had hoped for. If Finnivus had won the Battle of the Maw, he would have put each and every shark that opposed him on a feeding platter.

That Tydal, a lowly epaulette shark, had been chosen to lead was nothing short of incredible. Finnivus had no children, so after his death the main royal families—Punjaw, Razor Tooth, Charavyuh, Korak, and Taj—each thought they were the best fins to lead Indi Shiver. But they were all equal in power and none would ally with another. They couldn't agree, so when Gray picked Tydal—probably as a joke—they said yes.

Tydal knew the royals chose him as a placeholder— he'd even heard them use that word—destined for the Sparkle Blue as soon as any of them won the power struggle for control. The royals considered him a mucksucker because epaulette sharks preferred hunting squid and shellheads by the seabed instead of catching fish in the open waters. There was no way any would allow themselves to be led by a mucksucker. But Gray was too smart for them. He had kept the Indi court—including the strongest of the royal sharkkind—in the Atlantis and under guard as "guests" until Tydal could sort things out. What Gray hadn't counted on was that the royals were getting messages to their relations in the Indi homewaters.

It was those sharkkind who had made the attempts on Tydal's life. The most recent was by a squaline, one of his own personal guards. It was only the lightning quick reaction of Xander del Hav'aii, the AuzyAuzy commander and a royal himself, that had saved Tydal's life. Xander had relieved the squaline of their duties, and now Tydal was guarded only by AuzyAuzy sharkkind.

Tydal wondered if that made his chances of survival better or worse. The AuzyAuzy homewaters had been destroyed by Finnivus and Indi mariners. For better or worse, he was an Indi shark. What did any of them care if Tydal lived or died?

Enough moping, he told himself.

Tydal was Indi's acting leader and there was work to do. Though his selection was approved by the royals because they thought him weak, he still had to rule them. It was the only way that Indi wouldn't get into another war. The royals had been coddled their entire lives. Most didn't understand what it was to be told they couldn't do anything they wanted. Each thought everyone should bow before them, just like Finnivus. They were dreadful! If Tydal allowed one of the royals to take his place, there would be plots and killings and finally civil war.

I cannot allow that, he thought. We have been through too much already.

Tydal swam out from the gardens and into the royal court proper, where Indi's coral throne sat. The throne was made of gleaming rose coral and polished by sea snails until it shined. When the sun above the chop-chop cast its rays just so, the reflection formed a rainbow that glowed around the throne like a halo.

Tydal didn't like resting his fins on the coral throne. It felt haughty and arrogant. Then there was the fact that whenever he did so, absolutely nothing got done because the royals grew angry by what they thought of as arrogance when he used it. They challenged him in every small way that they were able. It shouldn't have been the case since Tydal was their chosen leader, but there it was.

"Giving it another go today, are we?" Xander asked. "Do I need to call in more of my mariners?"

"I think you have enough," Tydal replied.

The scalloped hammerhead always looked like he was thinking deeply because of the ridges in his oddly shaped head. Tydal knew Xander was smart but he could also be rude and unhelpful because he hated being stuck in the Indi homewaters. But the hammerhead had recently saved Tydal's life, so that was a big point in his favor.

"Try not to let them snout-bang you so much, mate. It gets boring watching you used and abused every day by this sorry lot, savvy?"

Tydal searched the hammerhead's eyes to see if he was joking or making fun. It seemed that he was actually offering advice. Truly, Xander was a mystery.

Tydal nodded to indicate to his own First Court Shark, a port jackson named Oopret, to put the royal court in session, which he did by saying, "The Indi Shiver royal court under Minister Prime Tydal, the first of his name, is now in session. Swim forward and be heard!"

Five sharks, one from each of the royal families, came forward in a group. Usually they jostled one another for the chance to speak first. Sometimes there was a big enough fight that Tydal could simply cancel the audience, which was always a relief.

This silent grouping was new and couldn't be good.

The tiger shark from the Taj family glanced right and left before speaking to Tydal, who hovered by— but not on—the Indi throne.

"Minister Prime, we representatives of the five royal Lines demand to know what you're doing to free our kin from their unlawful and illegal imprisonment in the Atlantis!"

So that's it, Tydal thought. They're working together.

Bringing their princes and princesses back to Indi would set all of their war-mongering plans into motion, and Tydal would surely be killed. He would have to be an absolute dunce to do this so it wasn't going to happen.

"I'm having high-level talks with Striiker, the leader of Riptide, and Graynoldus Emprex, the Seazarein, to do just that," he lied. "When I know something for certain, you'll be the first I inform."

"So, you know nothing . . . for certain?" asked the spinner shark from Korak. He left a huge pause between the words *nothing* and *certain* on purpose.

On the outside Tydal remained serene. He had learned well to keep his face free of emotion, especially negative ones, in Finnivus's royal court. "No, I didn't say that. I know many things about that topic that are very certain, but I cannot tell you what they are at this time."

"So you're keeping this information to yourself?" wailed an ancient Razor Tooth princess. "I have no idea what's become of my grandson and I'm worried sick!"

Tydal knew this wasn't the case. The old crone and the prince hated each other. There were even rumors that she'd tried to have her grandson sent to the Sparkle Blue using an urchin king assassin.

"I know it's been hard on you," he told the group.

"He loves ruling over us!" cried out the Razor Tooth princess. "I bet he'll have them put to death to stay in power!"

"That's not true!" he shouted. Though it would solve his problems, Tydal couldn't send those sharkkind to the Sparkle Blue like Finnivus would have done. He didn't want to be anything like Finnivus. But Tydal's voice was drowned out as the five royal representatives all began yelling.

The Taj shark's voice overcame the others. "You've

betrayed us and now are allied with Graynoldus, the very shark who sent our beloved emperor to the Sparkle Blue! You're a traitor!"

Tydal couldn't believe it. Beloved emperor? Each of the royal families had lost members to Finnivus's temper. He had even eaten the heads of a few in front of the royal court while their families watched! "Are you insane?" Tydal sputtered.

Xander streaked in and rammed the Taj shark in the flank. The other four sharkkind from the royal families clammed up as the Taj royal writhed in pain. "You dare touch me?" he gasped.

POW! Xander whirled and hit the Taj shark again with a huge tail slap to the face.

"Not only do I dare touch you, I can do it anytime I want. True it's not as fun as sending your princes to the Sparkle Blue in the battle waters, but it'll have to do. And let me tell you another thing, the next sharkkind that mentions the beloved emperor Finnivus won't live to say another word! You pack of krill-faced jellies savvy that?"

The group of five sharkkind collected themselves and left without another word.

Tydal swam down to Xander. "That was fantastic! I can't believe you did that!"

The hammerhead turned and his eyes blazed. "I wouldn't have to if you were any kind of leader! Might as well put an empty conch shell on that throne for all the good you're doing." With that, the scalloped hammerhead pushed past him.

"What? What did I do?" asked Tydal, bewildered.

But Xander was already gone.

CHAPTER 6

GRAY HAD SET OUT FROM FATHOMIR TO THE
Sific Ocean and AuzyAuzy Shiver soon after his visit
with Trank at the Stingeroo Supper Club. It sounded
like there was something going on in the eastern fire
waters, and he had a bad feeling that Hokuu was behind it.

Gray brought Barkley and Mari along and was glad
of it. When they reached the AuzyAuzy homewaters,
the official welcoming ceremony was incredible. There
were races and synchronized swimming displays and
everyone ate course after course of delicious fish.
Gray had wanted both of his friends with him because
he valued their advice. But in Mari's case, he wanted
the thresher along to keep an eye on her. She hadn't
been the same after the destruction of the Riptide
homewaters and he was worried about her. Here Mari
seemed to be enjoying herself more than she had in

a while. Shear was also around, watching Gray with his invisible finja guardians, but didn't call attention to himself.

Gray was a little annoyed that he didn't get to join any of the activities. Judijoan had made it clear that as the Seazarein he couldn't be playing Tuna Roll or Capture the Golden Greenie when visiting the ancient shivers. "It's not dignified," the oarfish sniffed.

Apparently being dignified meant you had much less fun.

So while Barkley got to win a game of Capture the Golden Greenie for his team, Gray hovered with Kendra, the whitetip shark who was regent and who had led AuzyAuzy Shiver ever since King Lochlan died fighting Finnivus. The captain of her guard, Jaunt, was also there, though, and she was always fun.

Finally, after hours and hours of watching the ceremonial celebrations, Jaunt took Gray to the area where AuzyAuzy's Eyes and Ears had their base of operations.

"Everything going well with you?" Gray asked Jaunt as they swam to a reef section in the homewaters.

"Sure, I reckon things have smoothed out a bit since the scrumble with Indi Shiver and Finnivus," she answered. "A hard current that was."

"Yeah, hard current." That was an understatement.

"This Hokuu seems like a rotten squid carcass," she said. "You think Leilani can help?"

"Maybe. What do you know about her?"

"Oh, she's lovely," Jaunt said. "We've been pals since we were finbiters. Don't get out with her too much these days because the Eyes and Ears keep her close. She's brill at what she does, is why they do that."

"So who leads this spyfish group?" asked Gray.

"A finner named Benzo," Jaunt said. "Everyone calls him BenzoBenzo."

"Why's that?" asked Gray.

Jaunt chuckled. "See if you can guess. Here he is now."

The fattest blowfish Gray had ever seen swam out to meet them from underneath a shelter of intricate blue and green coral. His giant face went directly into his tapered body which had yellow and brown markings on top along with spiny knobs all over his body.

"Ah, you're here, you're here. It is an honor to meet you, Seazarein Graynoldus, and I greet you as the leader of AuzyAuzy Shiver's Eyes and Ears, Eyes and Ears."

Gray gave Jaunt a look as they both stifled a snicker. "Hail and well met, BenzoBenzo. May the currents be warm and always at your back."

"One can only hope, but there's distressing news for those who know how to watch and listen, watch and listen." The blowfish waggled his fins back and forth.

"I'll leave you two alone," said Jaunt. "Have to check on Kendra's guard detail. Say hi to Leilani for me. And Gray, don't be a stranger." The small tiger shark turned smartly and with a final tail waggle was gone.

"Ah, yes," BenzoBenzo said. "Leilani, please attend us, attend us."

A spinner shark came away from her conversation with a few other sharkkind and dwellers. Leilani was slender with a pointed snout. She was a bronzed gray on the top and had a short dorsal fin that was only as high as the top half of her graceful tail, which was larger on top than bottom. She beamed at Gray with her narrow, triangular teeth. "Wow! The Seazarein! I never thought I'd get to see you up close."

BenzoBenzo rolled his eyes. "Leilani, what have I told you about meeting fins of importance?"

"Oh, right." She dipped her cute—Gray couldn't help but notice—snout. "I greet you, Seazarein. How may I serve the leader who represents the good and goodly fins of the Big Blue?"

"Ugh, please," Gray told the pair. "Forget the formalities. Have you heard anything about Hokuu?"

BenzoBenzo shook his enormous head. "Unfortunately, no. We have no verified leads, verified leads."

Gray flicked his fins. "Your patrol went missing in the same area where there have been a series of unexplained disappearances. Have Kendra or Jaunt sent others there since the ones you reported to me?"

The blowfish shook his head. "Regent Kendra thought it too dangerous. The fire waters in that area have been curiously active, curiously active."

Gray despaired. The fire waters were dangerous at the best of times. Maybe the missing scouts and Trank's spies were just unlucky. "So, there isn't anything that would lead you to believe that Hokuu might be there?"

"Nothing verified as of yet, as of yet," BenzoBenzo said.

"What about the flashes?" asked Leilani.

The leader of the Eyes and Ears spun his stubby flippers in annoyance. "Leilani, that is unconfirmed, unconfirmed!"

"What flashes?" Gray asked, curious.

"One patrol that was scouting the territory about a mile away from where the other disappeared did report that they saw blinding flashes of color. They took a closer look but when they arrived, nothing was there," Leilani said.

"Which is why I told the Seazarein that nothing has been verified or confirmed, verified or confirmed!" BenzoBenzo exclaimed. "That could have been anything: reflections of the moon above the chop-chop, volcanic activity, a colony of lumo jellies, glowing plankton, or even ghost shimmer. You cannot bother the Seazarein with wild theories! That's not what we do, not what we do."

"I'm sorry," the spinner said, her tail drooping. "It's just this Hokuu is a master of shar-kata, like Takiza, and I thought . . ."

BenzoBenzo sucked water into his mouth with a *shooop* and quadrupled his size in anger. Now the blowfish was totally round and the knobby spikes covering his body revealed themselves as long and sharp. "Leilani, be quiet! Be quiet!"

Gray cut his tail through the water. "Let her speak! And? Go on," he told the spinner.

"It's well known that Takiza can gather the power of the tides with his mastery of shar-kata," she began. Leilani unconsciously swam back and forth as if she were lecturing a class. "When he does, a bright glow gathers because of this concentrated energy. The description I received from our patrol would rule out moon reflections, ghost shimmer, lumo jellies, and plankton. Volcanic activity can be that bright, but it's almost always red, orange, or yellow. This was a bright green color, described as blinding."

"Could you lead me and a few others to where these flashes happened?" Gray asked.

"Yes, I have complete knowledge of the fire waters as well as every other ocean," Leilani said. "I'm also an expert on prehistores, ancient legends, landshark objects in the Big Blue, and can translate most dolph and orca whistle-click-razz dialects."

Gray turned to BenzoBenzo. "I'm going to need to borrow her."

The blowfish sighed, releasing the water he had gathered into his body and deflating to normal size. "I was afraid you were going to say that, going to say that."

CHAPTER 7

SNORK CHURNED HIS TAIL AS HE BALANCED THE rounded piece of coral perched on his bill. He had to constantly shift position left and right as the choppy current kept threatening to knock it off.

Takiza floated serenely off to the side but still in his vision. "Breathe," the betta said.

"I—am—breathing," Snork gasped.

"Breathe . . . better," the betta emphasized.

What did that even mean? thought Snork.

Takiza had said to come with him to a huge coral reef outside the Fathomir homewaters. Snork liked being included in things. And he had never had a private conversation with the great Takiza. He was so surprised and excited he said yes without asking why.

He definitely should have asked why.

Takiza gestured with one of his delicate and colorful fins. "Toss the coral upward. While it is above your bill, cut down a single stalk of greenie and then catch the coral once more. Repeat this until I tell you otherwise."

Snork flipped the coral up a few feet and then used his sharp bill to cleanly chop a stalk of kelp in half. He gathered the coral onto his bill. After taking a moment to balance it, he did this again.

"Faster," Takiza said. "Speed and precision are the hallmarks of a bladefish."

Snork kept throwing the coral above his bill and severing the nearest stalk of greenie, all the while moving forward. It was difficult.

"You . . . are not terrible at this," Takiza remarked. "Have you ever done this particular exercise before?"

"Not—on—purpose!" Snork answered as he fought the current to keep the smooth piece of coral from falling off his flat bill. "Sometimes . . . when I didn't do my chores . . . Dad would . . . make me do this as punishment."

"Intriguing. Your father trained you as both a reward and punishment. Something to consider with my next apprentice, perhaps. Now, catch this second piece of coral on your bill without dropping the first," Takiza told him before zipping away.

"What?" Snork asked.

He understood seconds later when Takiza somehow flipped a larger chunk of coral high above him. It dropped through the water toward Snork, but to the right. There was no way to catch them both unless he moved. Snork flipped the first chunk of coral upward and to the right. He caught the second as it fell, then recaught the first.

His dad always said he was pretty quick with his bill.

The weight was terrible though, and Snork thought his eyes would pop from his head.

"I did not say you should stop cutting down greenie," Takiza remarked.

Once Snork got the two pieces of coral next to each other, he resumed cutting stalks of kelp. "This—is—hard," he sputtered.

"That is because it is not meant to be easy." Takiza floated above one of the chunks of coral as Snork adjusted his position to keep both pieces on his bill. "Your father was a bladefish. It is the only reason for you to have experience with these exercises. He was training you with the games that you played, as well as the punishments you received."

The current died around him and Snork smoothly sliced a thicker strand of kelp. He hesitated for a moment as memories of his father flooded into his mind. Takiza somehow knew that both Snork's father and mother were swimming the Sparkle Blue. It had happened a long time ago, before Snork met Striiker, Shell, and Mari and before they all formed Rogue Shiver with Gray and Barkley. He missed his parents so much, but he was sure that their spirits had led him to meet his very best friends in the world.

"He—he never said anything about that," Snork said, striking at a piece of purple-greenie. "What's a bladefish?"

Takiza's fins billowed in all their colorful rainbow glory as he spoke. "Bladefish are a secret society of wandering warriors—sharkkind and dwellers—who swim the seven seas and right wrongs. Now, catch the third piece of coral without dropping the first or second, and of course, continue cutting greenie." The betta zipped away and flipped another piece of coral—this one larger than the first two put together—to Snork's left.

"Aw, krill!" Snork exclaimed as he thrust his bill up hard, launching the two pieces of coral on it to the right. But the third chunk of coral was heavier and fell too fast. It hit him right in the head . . . followed by the second, then the first. "Oww!" he cried.

"It seems there is room for improvement," the betta said. "Your training is advanced, but incomplete. We will have to remedy this."

"How come I've never heard of these bladefish?" Snork asked, shaking his aching bill from side to side and taking a much-needed breather. "I mean, how come my dad never told me?"

"As to the latter, you were too young. As to the former, I did say it was a secret society. Bladefish do not reveal themselves as bladefish. They do not seek glory." Takiza paused, thinking for a moment. "I must correct myself. Most do not seek glory. Most simply solve whatever problem needs solving and continue on their way."

"That sounds . . . awesome!" Snork said, whipping his bill back and forth in the water. He stopped and turned to Takiza. "But it can't be true, about my dad, I mean. My dad never went on adventures. He never went anywhere. He stayed with me and my mom."

"Yes, he would have," Takiza said, nodding. "Bladefish are loyal and true. I suspect your father met your mother, promised himself to her, and then you came along."

Snork liked the story. And his father had loved his mother. That was definitely true. He thought back to the last time he had seen his father. Their shiver was being attacked. Even though his dad wasn't in the Line, he was right at the front of the fighting. Then it was all chaos . . . Snork swam and swam. He didn't know how long he was alone before meeting the first of his friends. He had been very young.

"Are you going to train me to be a bladefish?" Snork asked in wonder.

"I cannot," Takiza said. "A bladefish must be trained by another bladefish. Oh, it pains me, but there is only one fin for this job."

"Who's that?" Snork asked.

Takiza was about to answer when a flying fish darted to a stop in front of the betta. The flying fish flicked his glittering fins in a downward salute. "Quickfin Speedmeister with a message for Takiza Jaelynn Betta vam Delacrest Waveland ka Boom Boom from the Seazarein, Graynoldus Emprex, lord of the seven seas, master of the five oceans—"

Takiza slashed his tail through the water. "Can't you see that I am ages old? Please get to the message while I am still alive to hear it."

Snork watched as Speedmeister—what a cool name!—continued."Yes, honored Takiza! Code word: Orange Roughy. The message is as follows—"

The betta shook his fins once more. "I assume this is a private message." Takiza pointed with his tail at Snork.

"Oh my, yes! Sorry!" the quickfin messenger responded. "I just get so excited. I love this job!"

Snork couldn't hear anything after that. He could see Takiza nod, frown, and then frown some more. He told Speedmeister something and the flying fish sped off in a blur.

"Bad news?" he asked.

Takiza sighed. "It seems your training will be continued at a different location."

CHAPTER 8

THE FIRE WATERS BLAZED TO HOKUU'S LEFT AS a gout of lava blasted from the seabed before being snuffed out in a sizzling hiss. He reached out with his senses. The ground below trembled with seaquakes, causing some of the giant rock spires nearby to crumble and fall. The barrier between the Underwaters and the Big Blue was weak here.

This would be the spot.

Here is where a new watery world order will begin, Hokuu thought.

His thoughts were interrupted by one of his captains, Freya, a mako finja. "This place gives me the creeps," she said.

Hokuu gazed at the prehistore mako. Freya was an excellent predator, one of his most reliable mariners. She had betrayed the former Seazarein, Kaleth, at the flick of his tail. Her loyalty was unquestioned.

Freya had vowed to lay down her life for his cause along with each and every one of the fifty or so mako finja who were left from the original group. Just like frilled sharks, makos had been mistrusted since the time of Machiakelpi, who had swum with Tyro and First Shiver. Hokuu had promised an end to that. He had promised that they would never be looked down upon again, that they would be important.

Hokuu would keep his word. Now was the time he would make good on all his promises.

"Gather the others," he told her. "I have something to tell them." The finja left to spread the message.

Hokuu saw a flare of orange brilliance as another stream of molten rock brightened the waters for an instant. It was all coming together. After years of frustration, he would succeed in a matter of days. There had been so many delays, mostly caused by the massive challenge of creating a passageway to the Underwaters large and sturdy enough for a prehistore to use. The power he exerted with his mastery of shar-kata wasn't enough to do it properly. Other times his setbacks were caused by Kaleth, Takiza, and even the insolent pup named Gray.

But Kaleth, the former Seazarein, was dead, and it was Hokuu's tri-tipped teeth and spiked tail that were responsible. That victory had been sweet. Takiza would have also fallen but the little puffer fish had wriggled from his coils. Hokuu's muscular body rippled in frustration at the memory. It would have been good to rid himself of that nuisance.

His old apprentice didn't have the strength to match him, but Taki did possess a cunning and devious mind. Unfortunately, Hokuu himself had taught him some of that. No matter. The betta would swim the Sparkle Blue. And Gray, or Graynoldus, as he was being called now, was less than nothing to Hokuu. As if the fat pup could ever be the true Seazarein! He might be able to lead a drove of weak-minded fish to a few victories, but that was it. Hokuu could send the pudgy shark to the Sparkle Blue anytime he chose. If he and Taki came around now, well, they would get a nice surprise. This made Hokuu smile a bit.

Freya returned with the other mako prehistores and all gathered as a large seaquake shook the ground below them. A few of Hokuu's mariners had to dodge a volcanic rock pillar that crumbled behind them. The weather in the fire waters was superb today! Hokuu took this as a favorable sign that the current he was on was the right one.

"The makos were the only fin'jaa from the Underwaters who understood that this world is a pale reflection of our shining past. The others—the tigers, the great whites, the hammerheads, blues and bulls, threshers and spinners—all of them, they shrank from the truth like turtles. The Big Blue is broken!"

"Hail, Hokuu!" cried Freya, and the other makos joined in with a throaty yell.

He rippled his body in an intricate pattern, which was his way to draw power from the water. In a moment he began giving off a soft glow. "To heal the Big Blue . . . we must destroy the pretenders who rule it today. To do that I must free our allies from the Underwaters!"

There was more cheering and Hokuu waited for it to die down. All the while he stole more and more energy from the ocean around them. Hokuu glowed brighter still because of this and soon he could see his reflection dancing in the black, black eyes of Freya and every other mako before him.

He dropped his voice. "But to free Drinnok and the others of Fifth Shiver requires more power than I can take from the waters, more than I can call with shar-kata. It requires sacrifice . . . from all of you!"

Some of the finja cheered. Others went silent. Many were confused. That was to be expected. They couldn't understand how his vision of the future was to be made reality.

Hokuu filled himself as much as he could with the power of the waters and grew incandescent. He reached out and touched each one of his mariners. A few tried to turn and protect their eyes but found they could not. This wasn't shar-kata, but dark-kata. It was a different and more powerful way of gathering power, not from the waters but from the life force of living things.

"Free Fifth Shiver so we can make everyone here suffer!" Freya shrieked.

Hokuu smiled at her. "You've always understood the concept of sacrifice, Freya. A better mariner has never gone to the Sparkle Blue."

Freya preened, soaking in the compliment as if she were feasting on a scrumptious bluefin tuna. Then the mako realized that she couldn't move. "What is this, my lord?" she asked.

"I thank you all for your loyal service," Hokuu told the mako finja. "Drawing power from the waters isn't enough to free the prehistores. I must have your strength!"

There were no cheers this time. The makos stared in stunned silence.

Hokuu sent his dark-kata lines of energy into the makos, into their powerful hearts and muscles, then sucked it greedily into himself. The mighty prehistore finja aged in front of his eyes as he stole their life force and made it his own. They crumpled, their flanks caving in, their smooth skin cracking and flaking as their energy was added to Hokuu's own.

Freya was strongest and lasted the longest. She was able to scream, "But—I love you!" before she too was nothing but a husk.

The current swept their remains away.

Hokuu stabilized the power raging inside his body

before he answered, "I love you too, Freya. I love you all."

And then, making sure he was in the correct spot, Hokuu created a beam of power that bit into the seabed toward the Underwaters. Toward glory and the future!

CHAPTER 9

"IT'S TOO QUIET," SHEAR MUTTERED FROM HIS position above Gray. The big tiger insisted on guarding Gray's dorsal fin as they swam in the fire waters searching for Hokuu. Sometimes it felt like the captain of his guardians was riding on Gray's back, which was supremely annoying.

"I think it's nice," said Leilani. The spinner shark twirled herself in the water. "I didn't picture the fire waters being this calm."

"They aren't usually," Gray told her, moving a little to his left. Shear matched the move, of course. "And I thought you knew the fire waters well."

"I do," Leilani said. "I memorized every scout report and put together a complete map in my head." She grew a bit embarrassed. "It's just the first time I've actually been here. First time I've been outside AuzyAuzy territory, in fact. Ohh, that's stink greenie!

It only grows in the fire waters and they say it's the worst smelling greenie in the entire world."

Barkley gave Mari and Gray a grin as they watched Leilani swim around and through the copse of bright red greenie, sniffing it, her eyes wide. "It's true! Oh, this is terrible! You guys need to smell this! It really stinks!"

"So, she's excited to be out," Barkley noted.

"Looks like," Gray agreed as he took in the calmness around him. "The water is still here."

Mari flicked her fins in agreement. "It's like there's no current at all. Weird."

Shear scanned the distance for danger. "I don't like it." His stomach was now resting on the tip of Gray's dorsal fin.

Gray moved to the side. "Shear, why don't you enjoy the calm before the flashnboomer? I'm sure something will spoil it soon. Until then, relax."

Barkley smirked to Leilani when she rejoined them, pointing at the muscular prehistore finja. "He's always on edge." The dogfish then did a pretty good imitation of Shear. "I don't like it. It's too quiet— there's too much greenie—not enough greenie—too cloudy—too sunny—too watery!"

"Very funny," Shear said, not amused.

"Admit it," Barkley pushed. "There are no conditions you like swimming in."

"Incorrect. When I'm not guarding the Seazarein, I enjoy battling a cold, fast current," Shear answered from directly above, again grazing the tip of Gray's dorsal fin with his stomach. "Good for increasing endurance. But when on duty, I prefer to be alert."

Gray poked Shear in the belly with his dorsal. "Could you be alert next to me? It's super annoying having you pressed on my topside like a barnacle. In fact, the Seazarein orders you to swim by his side."

Shear scowled but did as he was told. In an instant another finja had taken his place, though. "Oh, for crying out loud," Gray grumbled.

"Your dorsal will be protected or we turn around!" Shear insisted.

"Fine!" Gray shot back. He motioned to Leilani with a fin. "Are we near the area where the patrol reported the green flashes?"

As the spinner was about to answer, Mari pointed with her tail. "Look there! I see it!"

And there it was, over the next rise. The flashing green light had appeared barely two hundred tail strokes ahead. Shear motioned with quick fin and tail signals to his guardians and they faded into the water, almost invisible. It was a trick they could do, and it was difficult to spot them unless you were looking right at them.

"Seazarein Graynoldus, my guardians are in position to attack," the finja captain whispered. "I recommend you wait here."

"Shear, have you even met Gray?" Barkley asked.

"I've been with him since he was Kaleth's Aquasidor," the great white said, puzzled. "Did you hit your head on some coral when I wasn't looking?"

Gray snickered, but kept his voice low. "Barkley means that there's no way I'm staying behind. Especially if we're about to tangle with Hokuu."

"Um, Gray?" Leilani said and waggled her tail to get his attention. "That's not the right direction."

Everyone stopped. They looked from the flashing light to Leilani.

Finally Shear spoke. "It seems as if it is."

Leilani nodded. "I know. But the patrol saw the light over there." The spinner shark pointed in the opposite direction. "As you know, Seazarein Graynoldus, 'In case of an irregularity, it's best to base your decisions on the facts you do have.' That's actually a quote from Seazarein Stehli when he visited AuzyAuzy Shiver in ancient times." Her fins sagged a little as she lost confidence. "But the patrol saw the flashes there." Leilani pointed once more.

"Says the girl who's never been outside of her own homewaters as the bright green light flashes in the exact opposite direction," Barkley commented.

Shear waited for orders. Gray didn't want to dismiss Leilani's advice out of hand, but the evidence was rather glaring, in this case a flashing light over the next rise.

Leilani's tail drooped. "I know," she told everyone

finally. "I'm inexperienced and probably wrong. I'm sorry I spoke out of turn."

"It's fine," Mari said, giving her a tap to the flank.

Gray gestured to Barkley, Mari, and Leilani with a fin. "Why don't you three find a good place to hole up while we go in?"

"Gray, is it? Nice to meet you. My name is Barkley, and I'm going with you," his friend said.

Shear got the joke this time and snorted, "Oh. Good one."

Leilani also nodded. "I don't get out much so I'm coming, too."

The group crept to the edge of the rise. The waters were so still that Gray could hear sardines flitting in the scrub greenie by the seabed. The flashing light was there, but it ended about ten yards from the ground.

"That's odd," said Mari.

"I don't like it," Shear muttered. He noticed everyone looking at him because he said this so often. "Sorry."

Gray slashed his tail through the water. "We go in strong and straight at the light. Shear, have your mariners space out and let's Bull Rush right through the entire area in case Hokuu's masking himself. He won't stay hidden if we roar in there. On my signal."

Gray gave Shear a few seconds until the tiger finja motioned that his mariners were in place. He flicked his tail, and everyone moved forward in a silent rush. Oddly, he felt himself pass through a barrier of some sort.

The flashing green light disappeared and the current got rougher.

Suddenly there was a column of boiling water blasting up from the seabed instead of the flashing green light. The current became stronger. Much stronger. By the time they were ten tail strokes past the barrier, the water was pushing them off their swimming lanes.

"Swim through it! Swim through it!" shouted Shear.

But the current became so fierce it picked up the sand from the seabed and blasted everyone to the left. By then Gray knew he had made a terrible mistake.

They were caught in a whirlpool! It was a trap!

SPARKLE BLUE

CHAPTER 10

THE WHIRLPOOL WAS LIKE A FEROCIOUS BEAST. It pulled Gray and the others closer and closer to a scalding vent that spouted super-heated water from the seabed. This water was thick with sulfur and minerals that made him gag. Gray could feel himself getting woozy as it clogged his gills. In a few moments, he and the group would be unconscious and swept into the blazing geyser to be roasted alive.

"The current is too strong!" yelled Barkley.

"Swim with it!" Gray shouted over the rushing water and hissing bubbles. "Swim with it as fast as you can to the edge and break free!" He hoped the others had heard, although that seemed impossible. He would have to show everyone.

Gray powered his tail strokes left and right. With the speedy current, everything was a dizzy blur. He forced himself to the outside, where he saw Shear broke through along with two of his guardians.

Barkley dove closer to the seabed. Smart! The whirlpool was weaker there, and he pushed Mari free from its grasp.

Gray bumped another mariner to safety and then sped up as fast as he could to escape.

But then he saw Leilani!

She was tumbling snout over tail while being sucked toward the boiling water spout. He drove toward the sizzling center until he was past Leilani and then pivoted, churning his tail madly to keep from being dragged in. Gray would have one chance.

When the whirlpool brought Leilani around again, he swam with all his strength, crashing into her. He used his bulk to drive them both over the ridge that was the edge of the trap.

Gray and Leilani broke the invisible barrier with an audible *plunk* and tumbled into the calmer waters. He gasped, breathing in clean water. He looked over at Leilani, who was dizzy from her tumbling, but fine otherwise.

If he had listened to the spinner, they wouldn't have fallen into the trap. "You keep quoting advice whenever you want," he told her.

Leilani smiled, a little green around the gills.

Gray looked at Shear, Barkley, and Mari. Thankfully none were injured. "Shear," he called. "Report."

The great white dipped his snout. "Two of my

mariners were not able to evade the trap. Others have bumps but nothing serious."

Gray shook his head. Two more lives lost. When would it end?

"Did anyone else feel that barrier we crossed through before the whirlpool started? That was probably the trigger for the trap," Barkley said.

Leilani slapped her tail against a rock in frustration. "I should have put it together!"

Gray shook his head. "We were swimming too fast to stop."

Leilani turned to them all. "No, before that! The reason that the flashing light was in the exact opposite place it should have been is because it's being reflected! That's why the current was so smooth. Hokuu used his power to still the waters and reflect the bright glow of his powers."

"Very good!" shouted Hokuu from behind them.

Gray and everyone else turned.

The frilled shark flicked his spiked tail back and forth, smiling. "Oh, she's a keeper, Graynoldus. I mean, she would be if my friends weren't so hungry from their journey!"

The sharkkind of Fifth Shiver swam up from behind the frilled shark, and Gray's heart sank. Even though there were only about twenty of them, all were immense. Every one was a prehistore and much more mature than he was. Their hides were tough and thick, their teeth curved and sharp. Gray could tell from the way they swam that these sharks were the best of the best, battle-tested and ferocious.

There was no way his small group could hope to fend them off.

"Defensive positions!" yelled Shear. "Protect the Seazarein!"

One megalodon moved in front of everyone else. He was fifteen feet longer than Gray and a good deal thicker. "This is the Seazarein? This shark defeated your plans and kept us imprisoned? He's only a pup!"

Hokuu hissed into the huge megalodon's ear. "Yes, that is Graynoldus's son. He's the one who wants to keep you in the dark to be crushed when the Underwaters cave in. Strike quickly, King Drinnok, or he will surely slay you all!"

Gray swam forward, incensed. "That's not true, King Drinnok! I didn't even know about you until a few months ago!"

"Lies," Hokuu spat. "He lies every time he speaks! He'll never allow Fifth Shiver to live in the Big Blue! He wants you to stay underneath him until the Big Blue's floor falls onto your heads!"

"I swear by my father that's not true, King Drinnok!" Gray said. "We do not have to fight. There's plenty of room for everyone. Please, let's talk."

This gave Drinnok pause, until everyone heard:

"ATTAAAAACK!"

Five hundred AuzyAuzy mariners swept out from the side of a mountain range and straight at Drinnok and his prehistore mariners.

"See?" Hokuu shouted with glee. "He was delaying to gain time for his allies to arrive and destroy you!"

"NO! That's not true!" cried Gray as the lead sharkkind from the AuzyAuzy formation crashed into the prehistores.

"You will die for this!" shouted Drinnok. "I swear that by my father!"

The huge megalodon streaked forward to attack. Shear and three of his guardians rammed the giant prehistore, barely giving Gray enough time to dodge Drinnok's snapping jaws, which came together in a thundering crash.

Barkley skidded into Gray's flank. "We've got to go!" he yelled. Gray didn't want to leave. He knew he could make everything better if he could calm things down.

But then the megalodons blasted into the main AuzyAuzy formation, smashing through it and sending many sharkkind to the Sparkle Blue with ripping teeth and spine-shattering snout rams. Everything was chaos.

Still, he had to try!

"Stop!" Gray shouted to the AuzyAuzy mariners. "This is a mistake! I can end this! Stop fighting!" But there was no way to slow the frenzied battle.

"You don't give the give the orders around here, pup!" Hokuu yelled as he released a concentrated ball of power that zoomed toward Gray and Barkley.

There was no way to dodge it. There wasn't enough time to do anything.

Gray wondered what it would feel like to die.

But Mari flashed in front of them the instant before the bolt would have struck.

Her body was vaporized into nothingness.

"NOOOO!" roared Gray.

"Every single time!" Hokuu spat in disappointment. "Why won't you die?" The frilled shark sped forward and released a gout of green acid from his mouth.

A bright flash of power incinerated it. Hokuu was confused until he was blasted backward by another bolt of power.

It was Takiza!

The betta zipped in front of Gray and Barkley and shouted, "Flee, you fools!"

Takiza gathered power to fight with the frilled shark but Hokuu shouted, "Not today, Nulo! But soon! Very soon!"

The frilled shark whooshed away leaving a trail of bubbles.

"Mari!" Gray yelled as Leilani joined them. "Mari!"

"She's gone!" Barkley yelled in his ear over the din of the brutal fighting that continued all around him.

A megalodon came at Gray as he hovered in shock and indecision. Was Mari really gone?

Takiza touched the giant prehistore with a fin flick and paralyzed him. The megalodon crashed into the rocks behind them. "I said GO!" shouted the betta. "Shear, take them!"

With a flick of Takiza's tail Gray, Barkley, and Leilani were pushed a hundred yards away from the immediate fighting. Shear and his guardians rammed Gray to prevent him from turning back. "We must withdraw!" the tiger finja shouted in his ear. "It's a slaughter!"

Their retreat to the AuzyAuzy homewaters was dark and cold.

CHAPTER 11

THE FUNERAL WAS A SOMBER AND FORMAL affair. It was one level below the funerals of kings and queens and done after a special ceremony for the mariners that had been killed. Kendra had called for homewaters-wide attendance and bestowed the title of Loyal and Courageous Friend of AuzyAuzy Shiver on Mari. Gray thought this was well deserved but the honor, and everything else, tasted like ash in his mouth.

He was also angry at Kendra. She had saved their lives with her mariners but also caused the entire mess by ordering them followed. She'd wanted to make sure they were safe. Yet doing that, and then attacking when Hokuu and Drinnok threatened, had cost Gray a chance to solve the problem peacefully. He knew he shouldn't feel this way but couldn't help it.

There was no way to undo what had been done.

There was no way to bring Mari back.

The entire AuzyAuzy armada was arranged in two lines fifty sharks long, each facing the other with a swimming path down the middle. Every other AuzyAuzy mariner was stacked in rows of fifty directly above the first two rows facing each other. This formed a canyon of sharkkind whose heights stretched from the seabed toward the chop-chop. The path in between led to the Speakers Rock where Gray, Kendra, and other friends of Mari hovered. Behind the mariners, thousands of shiver sharks and dwellers watched. A school of humpbacks filled the waters with mournful whale song as a young thresher symbolizing Mari swam down the path formed by the AuzyAuzy armada.

Shear's face was set like rock as he and the other guardians hovered by Gray. Takiza's expression was neutral but Gray could sense the betta was hiding his true emotions. Jaunt and Leilani cried freely. Barkley tried not to do the same but was losing that battle.

Gray felt his body clench. He would love to howl in grief. But he was the Seazarein and had to be strong. The young thresher swimming down the path represented a new life taking the place of the one that had been lost. That may have all been true, but for Gray no one could ever take Mari's place. The thresher picked up speed and zoomed straight up toward the sun and the chop-chop. It was supposed to signify

Mari's passing from the Big Blue to the Sparkle Blue and it was beautiful.

But Mari's swim to the Sparkle Blue hadn't been anything like it! Gray trembled with anger and ground his teeth until one snapped off with a *kkrk!* Mari was burned to nothing by Hokuu! His vision turned red. All Gray could think about was biting into Hokuu's gills and ripping his head off.

One day he would. One day . . .

Suddenly Gray noticed the humpbacks had stopped singing and the only sound was the light current whisking past his ears. Everyone was looking at him. Kendra gently tapped him on the flank, her eyes filled with understanding. "Are you all right?" she whispered.

"Far from it," he croaked. Gray had completely forgotten that he was supposed to speak.

"You don't have to say anything," Kendra told him. "Mari would understand."

Gray shook his head. "No, I have to." He swam directly over the Speakers Rock of the AuzyAuzy homewaters. It was rare that anyone but the leader of the shiver got to speak from here. Kendra had told Gray that he could have done it today even if he hadn't the Seazarein. The whitetip was a good friend.

Gray took a deep breath and let it out, calming himself. He wouldn't rage about Hokuu here. He wouldn't turn this into a speech about vengeance because knew that Mari would have never wanted that. Not ever.

"Many of you AuzyAuzy mariners knew Mari because she trained and fought with us against Finnivus. Even though she was a fine mariner, Mari didn't send anyone to the Sparkle Blue during the battle against Indi Shiver's Black Wave armada. Instead she was one of the sharks who saved our wounded from a cold and lonely death as they spiraled toward the Deep Blue of the Maw. On a day that most of us would like to forget because of the terrible things we had to do, Mari shined. She came through it clean."

Gray surveyed the gathered sharkkind and continued, "Not many of you know this, but Mari is the only reason I'm in front of you today. My friend Barkley and I met her in the open waters. We were just pups and had never swum farther than a mile from our reef. She was with others who I got to know well afterward: Striiker, Shell, and Snork. Barkley and I were alone and scared and facing these four sharkkind who we didn't know. Neither group trusted the other, and after a short and tense conversation, we were about to go our separate ways. It was Mari who said, 'Wait. Don't go. Why don't we swim together?' She brought us together and helped us understand one another. She made us a shiver, and more than that, friends. That was Mari. She was special."

Gray took a moment to compose himself. His eyes

were welling up. In a matter of moments, he wouldn't be able to speak. "We've all been taught that when our loved ones go to the Sparkle Blue, it's a joyous time, not a sad one. And I'll try to be happy for Mari and not sad for me. But I can't help but feel that the Big Blue is … a little less bright today because she's gone. Thank you all for being here. She would have appreciated it very much."

Gray swam off Speakers Rock without making eye contact with Kendra, Barkley, or anyone else. He went down the path formed by the AuzyAuzy mariners as fast as he could without seeming like he was madly swimming away.

But there was no way around it. He was.

Gray had lost another one of his best friends and it felt like he would die.

Though he had duties as the Seazarein, he needed to be alone.

Just for a moment.

CHAPTER 12

VELENKA WAS IN A FOUL MOOD. SHE HAD BEEN dragged by Takiza and a few others to the AuzyAuzy homewaters against her will after the betta received a quickfin message from Gray. Takiza said she would be safer with them but Velenka knew he wanted to keep an eye on her. He didn't have to worry that she was going to make a break for it. With Hokuu sending as-sassins her way, she was content to be guarded by the Riptide mariners.

She watched as the mariners were dismissed and the rest of the shiver sharks and dwellers who had watched the funeral left. AuzyAuzy had increased the size of their mariner force since it had been savaged by Finnivus and the Black Wave armada. They were understandably worried about being attacked again. Now their mariners numbered almost a double horde, or two thousand sharkkind. It turned out to be a wise decision. Velenka had heard that AuzyAuzy had gone out with five hundred sharks against the megalodons from the Underwaters and lost one and a half droves. One hundred and fifty mariners would greet Mari in the Sparkle Blue.

Velenka was annoyed that she felt bad about Mari's passing. They had been rivals and even enemies since they were members of Goblin Shiver. Mari and the sneaky little dogfish, Barkley, had captured her trying to flee the Battle of the Maw. The thresher had been the one to show her mercy. Velenka doubted she herself would have done the same, given the opportunity. And Mari had been one of her only visitors when she was imprisoned in the Riptide homewaters. True, most of the time the thresher was digging for information, but their conversations had relieved some of her boredom.

Being so nice was probably an act, Velenka thought. No one was as noble as Gray had made Mari out to be. You didn't live long in the Big Blue if you were a softie. Velenka gnashed her teeth together hard after a sniffle escaped her nose.

Are you going to cry, you fool? she thought. Weakling!

"Beautiful, wasn't it?" asked a spinner shark, interrupting Velenka's thoughts. "I'm Leilani. I don't recognize you."

"That because I'm not from around here," Velenka answered.

"Where are you from?" Leilani asked. Her question seemed innocent but Velenka saw great intelligence in the spinner's eyes. Who was this Leilani and why was she so interested in her history?

"You've probably never heard of it," Velenka answered. "And yes, the ceremony was beautiful. Mari got herself a great send-off to the Sparkle Blue."

"You don't seem so broken up about it," the spinner declared. "Why is that? Don't you feel anything? You knew Mari, didn't you?"

Velenka swished her tail, acting unconcerned. It was best to seem relaxed when being questioned. "I did know her, but we weren't close. How is it that you feel so much? I saw you bawling like a pup and you couldn't have known her for more than a few days, right?"

Leilani shifted her position so she was looking straight at Velenka, now taking her measure. "The time I did know her I could tell that she had a kind soul. I've found you can tell a lot about a shark in a short period if you know what to look for, Velenka."

"And here I thought you were just another mourner, Leilani, but you know my name," she said. "It seems our meeting wasn't so random after all."

Leilani's eyes bored into Velenka, her act dropped. "Takiza made sure to inform Kendra and several others that you were here. After all, you swam with Finnivus and the Black Wave."

"I was forced to do that," Velenka answered automatically.

"Please, stop," Leilani told her. "Just know that Kendra isn't Gray. She won't hesitate to order an execution if she finds you're allied with Hokuu."

Velenka swished her tail and remained at ease. "I guess it's a good thing he's trying to kill me, then."

They stared at each other until Barkley slid into their view. "Well, this looks cozy. Are you two all right?"

"Couldn't be better!" Velenka answered in a faux happy tone. "I've got Leilani the junior spyfish interrogating me. That's what you are, isn't it?" She smiled at Barkley. "Makes me feel right at home."

Leilani's tail moved in short strokes, her temper coming through. "I meant no harm and of course, and I'm not here officially. I was curious to see if the stories I heard about Velenka being a demon fish were true. Turns out they are."

"Enough!" Barkley said, slashing his tail. "This isn't the time. Not here, not now."

"Fine by me," Velenka said, staring down Leilani.

The spinner met the gaze. "Me too."

Snork swam over to the group. He was clueless about what was happening, of course. "I wish Striiker could have come. He wanted to be here, but there's too much to do. It's so sad about Mari. I'm going to miss her but she's swimming in the Sparkle Blue with

Shell. Who knows? Maybe she'll meet my parents and say hi for me."

Velenka marveled that the sawfish had lived for this long in the open ocean. It didn't seem possible. He didn't possess an ounce of guile or cunning. He swam about smiling and clueless every single time she saw him.

"That's a nice thought, Snork," Barkley said. "It's the kind of thought everyone should have today. Right?"

The spinner shark ended her staring contest with Velenka. "Yes, it is. I'm going to leave so I can focus better on having those thoughts."

"You do that," Velenka commented as she left. Barkley gave her a look. "What? Can't you see I'm broken up and don't know what I'm saying? Please, give me a little current to swim in today of all days."

With that Velenka left, her mind a jumble of unwanted thoughts. If the AuzyAuzy Eyes and Ears were getting reports about her then the other great shivers probably had the same information. This was troubling. It would limit where Velenka could hide if she chose to escape. For all its vastness, the Big Blue was getting smaller each day for her. Soon there would be no place to hide without an enemy shark's teeth ripping at her gills.

I need to find a better current, Velenka thought. I need to change my life. But how?

CHAPTER 13

HOKUU WATCHED AS DRINNOK GAZED AT THE sun shining into the water from above. He and the other prehistores of Fifth Shiver had never seen sunlight before. When it had risen this morning, some went into a panic until their king calmed them. Most of the other prehistores from his shiver were hunting now but Drinnok had stayed with a wounded friend who had lost half of his right fin and hadn't stopped bleeding. That had attracted a few would-be predators who soon discovered that they were actually the ones on today's menu.

"I heard reports from Bollagan's scouts so I knew to expect brightness," Drinnok said of the sun. "But I didn't expect daylight to be so ... beautiful."

Hokuu curled his tail and pointed toward the chop-chop. "The sun shines for you, King Drinnok, and your holy mission to remake this ocean."

The megalodon scowled. "Bah! The sun burns now as it has done for all time, even though we did not see it. Do not think I'm some feebleminded fish to believe your flattery."

"Of course not!" Hokuu said. "I'm only trying to lift your spirits."

"Lift them by bringing more of my mariners from the Underwaters," he answered. "Though we are powerful, there are far too few of us to withstand an all-out fight against Graynoldus's allies."

"I am so sorry about that," Hokuu told the king. "My powers suddenly gave out. When I'm feeling stronger, I shall tunnel to the Underwaters once more."

Hokuu smiled inwardly. Actually, he had so much power from the life force stolen from his finja makos, he was fighting to keep it under control. It was pup's play to bore to the Underwaters now, and easier still to collapse his tunnel before too many of Drinnok's guard came through the passage. It wouldn't do to give the king everything he wanted. Drinnok might become unsympathetic to Hokuu's desires and that was to be avoided.

Hokuu slithered through the water so he was close to the massive megalodon king. "You must send Graynoldus to the Sparkle Blue, King Drinnok. Then you will be Seazarein."

What Hokuu really wanted was for Drinnok to kill the most beloved leader in the Big Blue. The megalodon king would have all sorts of enemies then. Hokuu would have to calm things by being named leader himself! But Hokuu could only lead after the Big Blue was conquered. And though he was very powerful, Hokuu couldn't do that alone. He needed an armada, and the prehistore mariners would only follow their king. Or someone in the Line after their leader's unfortunate death ...

"Crowns are earned, not given, Hokuu," Drinnok replied.

"Crowns are taken by those who are worthy," he told the king.

Drinnok grunted, acknowledging that truth. "Graynoldus's son—tell me more of him."

Hokuu spat. "An upstart pup. A bumbling usurper. The day you rid the ocean of him, the waters will rejoice!"

The megalodon king gazed at Hokuu before answering. "You told me that he led his forces to victory while outnumbered by a superior and better trained force—not once, but twice. I saw with my own eyes this AuzyAuzy Shiver come to his aid without question. And Kaleth, who was no fool, chose him to take her place as Seazarein. Graynoldus sounds like his father's son, not a bumbling usurper."

"He may have some small talent, along with a large current of luck, but he isn't a true Seazarein!"

Drinnok considered. "One victory can be counted

to luck. But twice? You underestimate him. It makes me wonder if you've given me an accurate image of Graynoldus."

Hokuu gnashed his tri-tipped teeth as his spiked tail swished back and forth. "How can you doubt me, King Drinnok? I freed you!"

"After a time," Drinnok noted.

"Because Graynoldus, Kaleth, and Takiza blocked me at every turn!"

Drinnok growled. "Takiza. That one. It's hard to imagine such a tiny dweller with so much power."

Before he could stop himself, Hokuu snapped his tail through the water with an angry craaack! "I will take care of that little puffer. He's no match for me, and besides, I taught him everything he knows."

Drinnok smiled. "That seems to have been a mistake. Back to Graynoldus. He did not immediately attack us. He wanted to speak of a peaceful solution."

Hokuu sputtered, "My—my king, I can't believe I'm hearing this!"

"Even if all of Fifth Shiver were brought to these waters along with the dwellers, we would still number far fewer than those who swim her presently."

"They are puny compared to any of you!" exclaimed Hokuu. "You can win!"

"Yes, but at what price?" Drinnok said, his voice rising. "What good is victory if there are so few of us left that illness or disease could wipe us out? It would mean the end of Fifth Shiver. That will not happen while I lead!" The megalodon calmed himself. "I must at least allow a chance for compromise."

"When Gray spoke, it was a trick!" Hokuu said, his anger rising. The king was being a fool. "You saw how his allies attacked when you hesitated. The Big Blue may not be as dangerous as the Underwaters, but one thing does remain the same. On any day, you can either have lunch, or be lunch. Which would you like to be, Drinnok?"

The megalodon swiped at Hokuu with his mighty tail, missing by an urchin spine. "I am the king. Remember that. What I command of you is to free more of Fifth Shiver from the darkness of the Underwaters. If you can't—or won't . . . we have a problem."

Hokuu relaxed his coils, straightening out his kinked and clenched body. He dipped his snout. "Rest assured, I will bring more of your subjects out from the depths."

Drinnok grunted and left. Hokuu watched the powerful megalodon swim away. Perhaps Drinnok, for all his size and teeth, wasn't strong enough to conquer the Big Blue. Hokuu twirled his long body, thinking. He couldn't expect the currents to be smooth while creating a new watery world, now could he? It was hard work and some days would bring frustration.

Like today.

But still, Hokuu would do exactly as he had been

asked and bring new and vibrant Fifth Shiver blood to the Big Blue. It would take a little time. Perhaps by then, Drinnok would see the error of his thinking and Hokuu wouldn't need to change his own plans. Perhaps Drinnok would realize that Gray, Takiza, and all the rest who opposed them had to be swept away.

Perhaps . . .

THE
UNDER-
WATERS

CHAPTER 14

GRAY, BARKLEY, LEILANI, SNORK, AND SHEAR crept over the rise and spotted the dark hole in the volcanic rock. The pale moonlight shining into the water cast everything in a ghostly white. "There," Leilani whispered. "Right where I thought it would be."

"Come then," Takiza said, floating above their group. "Let us see if this foolishness is even possible."

"What if Hokuu or someone is watching the hole?" asked Snork as he peered at the passage between the Big Blue and the Underwaters. "I know Drinnok and his prehistores were chased away, but what if they came back?"

"Hold a moment," Takiza told them as he gazed into the murky distance of the fire waters. Gray knew the betta wasn't looking with his eyes but stretching out with his other senses to detect if anyone was hiding nearby. Finally the betta said, "We are alone in this area."

"And my senses tell me that this hole doesn't go all the way through," Gray said. He could feel the other ocean far below but there was definitely some blockage between it and the Big Blue. His own senses, under Takiza's guidance, had become fine-tuned indeed.

The betta grunted approval. "Good, I see some of my training got through that thick skull of yours. But will you be able to move that amount of earth and rock?"

"I think so," Gray answered.

Takiza shook his head. "Do not think; do."

The group swam quietly to the ragged hole in the seabed that Hokuu had made to free Drinnok and the Fifth Shiver prehistores. "This is such a bad idea," Barkley said as he peered into the blackness. "How do we know it's not totally plugged?"

Leilani swam over the opening. "Because it's warm," she said. "The water is rising so it's not totally blocked. They say the water is warmer way below because it's closer to the ocean of lava that makes up the center of the world." She looked at the others. "That's only a theory, though."

A seaquake caused a crack to ripple across the seabed. Everyone looked at Gray, worried.

"I'm sure it'll be okay," he told them.

"I don't like it," Shear remarked.

"For once, I agree!" Barkley added and then looked

at Takiza. "If he's going to do this, shouldn't you give him some maredsoo?" Maredsoo was a type of deep-sea greenie that gave energy and warmth.

Takiza shook his fins. "Maredsoo can confuse the mind. It is not chilly in the Underwaters, and the pressure is only a bit more than here. Gray is strong enough to make the journey without it, provided he can break through whatever blockage there is between here and there."

Shear turned. "At least let me go with you."

Gray slashed his tail through the water. "We've been through this. If someone sees you, they'll think we're invading. No one will recognize me. That's the safest way. Besides, I don't know if I can get myself through, much less another set of fins. As the Seazarein, I'm ordering you to stay and protect everyone. That's how you can help me. I don't want to lose anyone else."

Barkley began, "Gray—"

"We'll talk later," he said. "I'll be five, ten minutes, tops."

"I think it'll take longer than that," Snork told him.

"I know, Snork. I know," he said. And with that, Gray launched himself upward and then curved down and into the passage to the Underwaters.

An hour later Gray was stuck fast. "Great," he muttered. "Just great."

Though Drinnok and most of the prehistores who came through days earlier were larger than he was, the tunnel had collapsed since then. It was probably the work of the nearly constant seaquakes that choked off the passageway. The mild current between the oceans allowed Gray to bore through even small openings, but now he was stuck. He was also exhausted. Though the distance wasn't so great, the constant twisting and turning he had to do was tiring.

"I'm not going to die in the dark," he told himself. Gray churned his tail and wriggled past the tight area. Physical strength wasn't going to work here. He needed shar-kata. His training on gathering energy from the waters around him had been going forward slowly. Takiza thought he wasn't making progress because he could solve most problems with his strength. That's why the prehistores from the Underwaters didn't have shar-kata. The surviving ones were all super-strong and didn't need it.

Gray concentrated, reaching out with his senses. He felt the energy all around him. In addition to being in the water, it was in the very earth. He didn't try to bend it to his will—he worked with it. Soon Gray was encased in a glowing shield bubble. There was water inside, of course. With a thought he extended and moved the dirt ahead of him. Gray swam forward, pushing the shield ahead. While he didn't have the strength to move the massive rocks blocking his way, shar-kata, along with the power inside the rocks themselves, did.

Finally, with one last push he popped into the Underwaters.

There was lumo light everywhere. It was kind of like swimming in water to which sea cow milk had been squirted. Gray went forward cautiously into the massive prehistore greenie. The fronds of some of the white plants were wider than he was. The stalks they grew from were also much larger than he had ever seen. All were a bone-white color from lack of sunlight.

Gray moved through the greenie, making sure he kept his bearings so he would know how to find the passage again. The water was warmer than the Caribbi Sea in the summertime. It tasted odd—Takiza had told him to expect this—but he could breathe all right. Gray shook his tail when it got tangled in some kelp and continued moving into the dense undergrowth where he hoped he would be well hidden from the large predators that were surely here.

Gray had half hoped that there would be some pressure change, or the different water would make each side weak or dizzy. Clearly this wasn't the case. If Drinnok got his armada into the Big Blue they would fight on equal terms.

Except that they're all giants, Gray thought, growing cold from that realization.

He tugged his tail free from a snarl of greenie. That was odd. He was being careful but had gotten his tail tangled twice now. Maybe there was some effect from the water even though he didn't feel it. Gray swam toward a brighter glow ahead.

He would have to go through a wall of the largest plants yet. These had huge bladders that swayed soothingly even though there was almost no current. There were fleshy sea flowers growing around these bladders. They looked and smelled delicious! Small fish were nibbling on them. Gray started thinking about a quick snack on some of the mouthwatering flowers but then chided himself. He didn't come down here to eat!

Get moving, fatso, he thought.

But he couldn't. Something was tangling one of his front fins. Gray saw that the greenie had somehow twisted around his left pectoral. At least that's what he thought until his right fin was grabbed!

It was then he realized . . .

The greenie was alive!

Gray swung his tail left and right to rip through the fleshy kelp but couldn't get enough force to free himself. Then the swaying bladders stopped swaying and turned toward him. It opened to reveal rows and rows of jagged spikes inside!

Gray struggled, ripping free his right fin, then his left. But now his tail was wrapped tight and he was being drawn backward toward the gaping mouth of the largest bladder pod.

I'm about to be eaten by prehistore greenie! swam through his mind.

"Oh, no, no!" said an enormous turtle who glided into Gray's view. His shell was as wide as Gray was long, and since the turtle was circular, that made this prehistore massive indeed. "I told you never to play in my garden alone. And you certainly shouldn't be feeding yourself to my plants."

"It's not my idea!" Gray said as he tugged against the greenie that drew him closer to the toothy bladder that was now snapping open and closed in excitement.

"Hold still," the giant turtle said as he stretched out his neck and clipped the greenie with his sharp beak. "I heard whispers you might be alive and here you are. It's good to see you."

"You know me?" Gray asked the giant dweller.

"But of course, little Gray!" the prehistore turtle told him. "Don't you remember me? My name is Barge and I used to look after you!"

CHAPTER 15

"LET'S GO THAT WAY," THE PREHISTORE TURTLE named Barge said, gesturing with a flipper. He was larger than Gray and his huge domed shell had bony spikes that were as sharp as volcanic rock. "There's less old-growth greenie there. The younger fields aren't as beautiful, but they are less likely to eat you."

"That's a big bonus," Gray replied. "I'm not used to greenie with teeth."

Barge clucked. "That's not the kelp's fault. It just wanted a meal, like you should. Look at you; you're so thin I can almost see through you. You haven't been eating properly. It's no wonder you didn't have the strength to pull free."

Gray had to smile. It took traveling down to the Underwaters to finally find a place where he was considered thin. Amazing. But he was on a mission to find out information. "Barge, there's trouble above this place in the Big Blue. Drinnok came through with some of his Fifth Shiver sharks and it looks like there might be war."

"I know," Barge said. "I'm on the dweller council. Nobody listens to me because I'm not a jurassic, but I do get to hear a few things."

Gray nodded. "Then maybe you can help me. I came down here—I don't know exactly why—maybe to find out what type of fin Drinnok is and whether there can be peace between us. Can you tell me anything that might be helpful?"

"I believe I can. Unfortunately I think everything circles back to the least favorite day in my long life," the turtle said with a frown. "The day I thought both you and Graynoldus died. I saw you and your father chased by the frilled sharks. Disgusting things, the frills. But quick. I could do nothing to help as I was too far away and I am rather slow. Sorry about that."

"That's all right." Barge seemed to need a sympathy pat so Gray thumped the turtle's rock-hard shell with his tail. "You've already helped me today and I'm sure there were other times when I was young."

Barge nudged Gray upward with a flipper as a different type of greenie shot up from below, trying to take a bite of his belly. "Nibblers," Barge explained as he gestured at a field of large white bulbs. "Their sting isn't that poisonous but they can take a chunk of you."

Gray shook his head as he looked at the (possibly deadly) greenie. "It's a wonder I'm alive at all."

Barge smiled and rubbed against Gray, pushing him a good twenty yards to the right. "Oh, you give yourself too little credit. I've heard what you've accomplished in the waters above. First Aquasidor, now Seazarein. A leader of fins and dwellers, beloved by all—"

"You must be confusing me with someone else," Gray said.

"Tut-tut! Don't interrupt," Barge scolded. "Elder speaking," he said, referring to himself with a smile. "You always did have a problem with that."

Gray dipped his snout. "I do apologize. Please continue."

"I rushed over as fast as I was able," Barge said. "There was a huge explosion and then a seaquake. No one came down from the passageway after that, not even any of the frills. The swimming lane was filled with loose rock and then lava sealed everything shut. It was horrible. Though Graynoldus was my best friend, many other good sharks, including King Bollagan, died that day."

"So, it was Drinnok who did that," Gray said. "I guess he has to be stopped."

"He may have to be stopped," Barge agreed. "But he was not responsible for the bloodshed that day."

"What do you mean?" asked Gray.

Barge gestured with a flipper. "Yes, Drinnok wants to leave the Underwaters. And he believes he deserves to be Seazarein. But he didn't kill King Bollagan or his Line. It was the frill sharks."

"Hokuu told them to do it," whispered Gray.

"Quite right," Barge agreed. "But they could not do it alone. They allied themselves with the jurassics and their terrible leader, a mosasaur named Grimkahn. The jurassics consider themselves better than all other dwellers. And they especially do not like being told what to do by sharkkind. They willingly allied with Hokuu. But after it was done, Drinnok was next in Line. He wasn't going to allow anyone else to lead Fifth Shiver. What was done was done."

Gray pondered everything he knew, everything he'd learned as Seazarein, before asking, "Is Hokuu on the Fifth Shiver Line?"

Barge nodded. "Now you have it. No, he is not. I believe that is the reason that Hokuu sent Bollagan and his Line to the Sparkle Blue."

Gray nodded, understanding. "That way if he serves Drinnok, he'll be named to the Line himself. Hokuu is using Drinnok to get into a leadership position."

Barge turned his large flippers. "This came up when Hokuu visited last. I watched from the side and said nothing."

Gray looked at Barge. "So if Drinnok doesn't do

what Hokuu wants then maybe Hokuu will use this Grimkahn and the frill sharks to send him to the Sparkle Blue, just like Bollagan. Even though Drinnok wants to rip my gills out, he has to be told."

Barge stretched his head forward and nodded, which exaggerated the movement. "I believe you are right. And then of course, if Drinnok is gone, Grimkahn or Hokuu would be in charge of who gets to come and go from the Underwaters. Not that it's such a big deal for me, but everyone should have a choice."

Gray looked around at the ghostly glow of the lumos. There were patches of milky light with darkness filling in the rest. It was hot, but not unbearable. Still, he couldn't allow the sharkkind and dwellers who lived in the Underwaters to be trapped here. He understood Drinnok's feelings about this clearly now. Perhaps through that they could find a common ground and avoid another bloody war.

"It'll take some time to get you all into the Big Blue," Gray said. "The passage barely lets me through. But I swear, I will come for you. Somehow, you'll all be saved."

Barge laughed, a musical rumble. "Graynoldus, you misunderstand me. It's the principle of the matter. It's not being allowed to leave that's wrong. But I don't want to go to your Big Blue. This is my home and I love it. Besides, who would take care of my garden?"

"You mean, who would save its victims if you left?"

Barge nodded vigorously. "That too! You'll find not everyone is so eager to leave. Sure, the young pups will want to take a look because it's new and it will annoy their parents to no end. But I think you'll find many will stay."

There was a rumbling seaquake. Gray looked up toward the lumo-encrusted roof of the Underwaters and then at Barge. "But I can't blame Drinnok or anyone else for wanting to get out of here before the roof falls down, can I?"

"Oh please," Barge said. "There have been seaquakes for millions of years and our world remains. That is a foolish thing for anyone to say."

"It's so dark, though," Gray said as he looked around. "Don't you want to really see? I can barely see anything."

"You're not used to it," Barge answered. "I'm sure that the Big Blue would be horribly bright for me. I get headaches if it's too bright, you know."

Gray gestured with a fin. "All the greenie and lumos are white! You should see how colorful it is in the Big Blue."

"What are you talking about?" Barge asked, confused. "The copse of taratellan greenie you were caught in was a riot of color! There was ghost pearl and alabaster and pale matte and glowmist and everything in between."

"Okay," Gray replied. "I'm not here to force anyone to do anything. But like you said, I want everyone to have the choice."

"Spoken like a wise and great Seazarein," said Barge with a smile. "Who should gain a little weight."

It took Gray the better part of three hours to wriggle and swim his way up the passage from the Underwaters to the Big Blue. And that was with the aid of sharkata, which thankfully seemed to be working pretty well. He met Shear close to two hundred yards from the end of the tunnel.

"I told you to wait outside," Gray said after he had caught up with the big tiger.

"Of course," he said. "I was guarding your friends until five minutes ago when I heard you coming. They are waiting."

Barkley, Takiza, Leilani, and Snork came out from their hiding places and crowded around as soon as Gray and Shear emerged from the passageway.

"Thank Tyro you're back!" Barkley exclaimed. "You're lucky you didn't get yourself killed."

"Agreed," grumbled Takiza. "Did you find out anything useful or simply bumble about as usual?"

"I met up with an old friend named Barge. He's a giant turtle," Gray told everyone.

Takiza nodded. He seemed to know Barge.

"What did he say?" asked Snork. "Anything good?"

Gray frowned. "No, not good. But I have a crazy idea on how to avoid a war with Drinnok."

"What would that be?" asked Takiza, swishing a gauzy fin.

"Talk with him," Gray said.

"That does sound crazy," Barkley nodded.

Shear frowned. "I don't like it."

"He's right," Leilani agreed. "Drinnok, or his guards, would eat you first and ask questions never. And then there's Hokuu. He'd never give you the time to convince anyone."

Gray nodded. "Yup. I need someone that Drinnok won't think of as a threat. Someone who could track him, find him, and sneak past his giant prehistore guards without getting killed. Then convince him we don't want a war. But there's no one in the Big Blue who could do all those things, I guess." By the end Gray was looking at Barkley.

"I like it," Shear said. "I like it a lot."

The dogfish flicked his fins, faking annoyance. "Maybe I should have kept my big mouth shut."

"It's dangerous, Bark," Gray said. "Really dangerous."

Barkley cut him off with a tail swish. "The risk is worth it. And you're right. I am the only fin for this job. And I'm going to do it well. And that's that."

And so it was.

CHAPTER 16

IN THE INDI SHIVER HOMEWATERS ON THE other side of the world, Tydal cringed as Xander shouted, "That Johanna fin was overheard plotting to kill you!"

"Please, calm yourself," Tydal said. "The princess explained that it was idle talk, a joke."

The furrows on the scalloped hammerhead's brow deepened in disbelief. "My mariners say it wasn't and I believe them. Besides, she's old enough to know better. No one gets to have a laugh about sending their leader to the Sparkle Blue, savvy?"

Tydal wished there was more room to swim so he could think, but the cavern was too small. The Indi homewaters were huge, but he and Xander were in a series of interconnected and defensible caverns in the royal area of the Indi homewaters. Xander had insisted on this after the latest assassination attempt. Now, even the few Indi mariners Tydal had kept around for public relations had been dismissed. All his guards were the AuzyAuzy commander's sharks. They were the only ones who could be trusted.

"Are you thinking or sleeping?" asked Xander, who knew well that Tydal wasn't sleeping at all these days. When Tydal was First Court Shark, he prided himself on being able to remain stock still, at the hover, for so long that he would fade from everyone's view. But that wasn't possible as minister prime. Everyone looked to you for answers and there was never a day with fewer than a hundred decisions to make.

"I cannot execute a Punjaw princess for mere words!" Tydal answered. "The family would revolt. In fact, all five of the royal clans might join together and then revolt!"

"Finnivus killed a bunch of them," Xander said. "Those same families offered to kiss his tail after each death."

"Because he was a maniac!" Tydal yelled, bumping Xander with his snout. Not too hard, as the hammerhead was far larger, but Tydal was angry. "Finnivus would have ordered Johanna's entire family wiped out!"

"Which is why they obeyed!" Xander answered forcefully, slapping Tydal in the belly with his tail. "They were scared of him. That's a lesson you should learn."

"You cannot be serious," Tydal said, shaking his head in disbelief. "You think I should put someone's head on a feeding platter to make a point? I will never do that. I won't be anything like Finnivus!"

"If you let her go without a fitting punishment, you're as good as dead," Xander said. "You know what? I'm done. The fate of the ocean is balanced on an urchin spine, and I have to play nurse shark with you. No more! You dying doesn't bother me."

Tydal used his tail to angrily sweep the seabed at Xander. "That's so great to hear! It inspires me with so much confidence!"

"Don't mistake me for your mum! I'm not here to stroke your flank." Xander calmed himself. "Hear me out. Yesterday, you were almost killed. Again." That was true. This last attempt, by three spinner sharks with fake Indi Shiver markings, had almost succeeded.

The evidence pointed strongly to the Punjaw family as they were in charge of the royal urchins who created the Indi Shiver tattoos. Unfortunately, there was no proof because all three assassins were sent to the Sparkle Blue before they could be questioned. Punjaw had loudly denied any involvement, but their princess Johanna had been heard laughing about how Tydal's rule was about to be "thankfully and finally put to an end" a day before the attack.

The hammerhead flicked his fins and said,

"This attempt on your life could have been random extremists, as your royals say ..."

"Xander," Tydal said. "I'm not an idiot."

"Then why are you acting like one?" Xander asked. "I lost another mariner saving your yellow-and-brown hide yesterday."

"I'm terribly sorry about that," Tydal said, suddenly conscious of his epaulette skin.

"Sorry gets nothing for his family," the shark told him. "He's gone and the royals don't respect you."

Tydal was hurt by Xander's words but he burst out laughing anyway. "Respect?" he gasped. "Who cares about respect? I care about doing what's best for the shiver!"

"The two are inseparable," Xander said. "You won't be able to lead, to help your shiver, if the royals don't respect you."

Tydal fell silent.

Xander was totally right. Tydal had been trying to govern by compassion and logic because he didn't think he was worthy, because he wasn't born into a royal family. But the truth was that the royals would never accept him no matter what he did—because they all wanted to rule. If Tydal was going to set a new course for the shiver he had to lead. He needed everyone to respect him and the position of minister prime.

"Are ya thinking or sleeping?" asked Xander.

"I'm awake, thank you very much," Tydal told the hammerhead. "Maybe for the first time as leader of this shiver. I need to make a royal proclamation, so everyone must be there. Will you gather the royal families?"

"What if they don't want to come?" asked Xander.

"Then escort them there," replied Tydal.

"With pleasure," Xander told him. "And I thought today was going to be boring."

"Xander," Tydal said, stopping the AuzyAuzy shark from swimming away. "Perhaps you should bring a few more sharkkind than usual. I don't think the royal clans are going to like what I say very much."

Xander dipped his snout to Tydal. "Now you're talking. I'll get it done."

The hammerhead swam out of the cavern yelling for his mariners.

Two hours later Tydal swam out to the coral throne at the heart of the Indi Shiver homewaters. Sunlight cut through the water and made everything around him sparkle. Tydal saw that in addition to tripling the guard in front and above the throne, Xander had also brought the rest of the AuzyAuzy mariner force. They were at a respectful attention hover and not talking and fin-slapping as they did from time to time when he held a royal audience.

Tydal aimed to set a regal tone from the start. He glided straight to the coral throne of Indi and plopped himself on it. A chorus of grumbles rippled through the royal court.

"Johanna Punjaw, come forward," Tydal said. The throne was the Indi homewaters' Speakers Rock. It was located in the place where the currents were the absolute best for carrying even a whisper out to the assembled royal court.

The noise from the court turned into indignant shouts: "What's the meaning of this?" "You dare order a princess around?" "He's not royalty!" And Johanna did not move. Tydal saw her, smirking, with the rest of the Punjaw clan hovering protectively around her.

Tydal gave a double fin flick to Xander, a signal they had worked out. The hammerhead bellowed, "QUIET! YOUR LEADER IS SPEAKING!" His commanding shout was so loud it silenced everyone.

Tydal edged forward. "Johanna Punjaw, come before me!" he announced, a bit harder this time.

The leading member of the clan swam out, a cunning old coot named Rash. He dripped disdain whenever he dealt with anyone but Finnivus himself. "The princess is too frightened to come before your imposing presence, Tydal," Rash said, words soaked in sarcasm. "I speak for clan Punjaw. Tell me what's bothering you. Now." The last was an order and caused a ripple of laughter from the royals.

"What I want you to do is produce the princess so she may defend herself," Tydal said. "She was overhead joking about my swimming the Sparkle Blue right before an assassination attempt that your clan are the main suspects in."

"We've been through that, Tydal," Rash said, not using his title of minister prime. "They were foolish words to say . . . out loud." More laughter from the royals because of the insulting pause in front of *out loud*.

"Your sarcasm and disrespect have been noted," Tydal told Rash. Anger flickered in the shark's eyes. He didn't like being called out. Suddenly the other royals went quiet. They became interested as Tydal continued. "Since your clan refuses to bring the princess forward to defend herself, I shall pass judgment on her, and your entire clan, solely from what I have heard from the other witnesses."

Rash's eyes blazed. "You pass judgment! You do not judge your betters, Tydal!"

"Silence him!" The words leapt from Tydal's mouth and he couldn't pull them back. Xander's mariners speared Rash in the flank and drove him nose first into the soft seabed, but thankfully didn't send him to the Sparkle Blue.

"How—how—dare you?" the old shark rasped.

Tydal propped himself up on the rose coral Indi throne and announced to the court, "The answer is simple enough that even a dumbo jelly like yourself should understand, but I will explain anyway. I dare because I am the minister prime and ruler of Indi Shiver!" Tydal paused. "Some of this misunderstanding is my fault. I haven't acted like a leader. I allowed petty sharkkind like yourself, who think they are better than the others because of a family name, to dictate terms. But no longer!" Tydal swam off the throne and directed his words at the Indi Shiver sharks. At least a thousand of them had gathered, hovering outside the royal court.

"From this day forward, being born into a certain family guarantees you nothing! You'll need to earn your position by demonstrating your loyalty to Indi Shiver. Not to a certain family, but to our noble and great shiver!"

"This is treasonous!" cried one of the sharks from clan Charavyuh.

There was grumbling and shouting. Again Xander swam forward and bellowed, "SHUT YER COD HOLES!" He then added in a quieter voice, "The minister prime isn't done speaking."

"There is treason here, that much is true, committed by Princess Johanna and the entire Punjaw clan!" Tydal said. "That is why I am banishing the Punjaw family. If any of their fifty-five clan members are seen in the Indi Ocean, they will be sent to the Sparkle Blue. Consider that your final warning! Captain of the guard, proceed with their banishment. Kill any who resist!"

Xander moved in with a hundred mariners, overwhelming the smaller royal family. This took several minutes. They screamed and cried but were pushed and bumped from the area.

There was a shocked silence in the court. Everyone stared at Tydal, who settled onto the rose coral throne. "Punjaw clan no longer exists as far as Indi Shiver is concerned. Their family name will be stricken from our history, any rights they have are voided, and their quarters are now the property of the office of minister prime. Any who think this is too harsh a punishment are welcome to swim forward and defend Punjaw. If you can convince me that I was mistaken then they can return." Tydal leaned forward and stared at the four remaining royal families. "But if you fail to make your case then you and your families will be judged allies of the traitorous Punjaw clan and banished also!"

Suddenly no one in the Razor Tooth, Charavyuh, Korak, or Taj clans felt like defending Johanna or any Punjaw.

"I take your silence as a sign that you all completely agree that every shark in the Punjaw clan is a traitor and deserved my just punishment. Good, excellent. It is done." Tydal looked down at the assembled royals. Those in the front were edging away and not meeting his eyes.

"Also, if any of you comes forward with information about traitorous activity anywhere in Indi Shiver, you will be rewarded. If you are accused by someone else, you must defend yourself to my satisfaction or you and your family will be banished. Failure to defend yourself will be taken as a sign of guilt and you will be banished also."

Tydal stared at the royal families. "So, is there any other business? Are there complaints about the way I'm handling things? Everyone was so chatty a minute ago and I'm all ears. Anyone? Anything at all?" He waited, allowing the silence to stretch out. "I didn't think so. You're dismissed."

And that night Tydal had his first restful sleep since he had been appointed leader of Indi Shiver.

CHAPTER 17

BARKLEY TOOK HIS TIME WORKING THROUGH the coral and greenie so no one would see him as he tracked Drinnok. Even so, he had rushed a little when going through the fire waters. He didn't like staying so close to the shifting seabed with all its seaquake tremors. One time, a gout of lava breached the surface fifty tail strokes to his left and exploded with a rumbling *BOOOOOM!*

It was pure luck he hadn't been right on top of it.

Barkley found Drinnok and the rest of the prehistores less than a day's swim from the AuzyAuzy homewaters. It wasn't hard picking up their trail. Drinnok and his mariners were all massive. They didn't need to hide from anyone, or even an armada of anyones. Most of them were around thirty-five feet and thicker and more muscular than Gray. And each of them had a tremendous appetite.

That was what gave them away. In every direction, large fins and dwellers were swimming for their lives, terrified. All you had to do was go in the opposite direction of the screaming survivors.

No, the problem wasn't finding Drinnok. The problem would be getting past his guards, who ate anyone that came too near. Barkley jammed himself into a crevice that was overgrown with greenie and watched. It didn't take him long to figure out the gaps in the patrol pattern. He waited until the sun was low and caused the most shadows before beginning his creep forward to the Fifth Shiver leader. If Barkley was spotted, there would be no time to explain himself or plead for his life. He would be gobbled up in one bite.

Well, you think you're the best at sneaking around, he thought. So prove it.

Drinnok rested himself between two coral reefs in the center of a ring of prehistore guards. The greenie in the area wasn't tall or as thick as Barkley would have liked, which was probably why they had chosen it. This kelp was more ropy than the leafy kind that would have hidden him better. Barkley positioned himself so the medium-strong current that pushed the green-greenie in Drinnok's direction was at his tail. This allowed him to move from one clump to another whenever heavier currents washed through the area. Slowly, he got closer and closer.

Barkley passed a giant thresher, who dozed after

having eaten an entire bowhead whale. The current pushed again and he darted to another clump of greenie. A prehistore bull shark turned. He had probably noticed something moving in the corner of his eye. The immense shark wasn't sure though. He poked at the greenie next to Barkley with his snout but then left.

Barkley moved once more, this time to a clump of greenie just ten yards from Drinnok's right flank. Two giant hammerheads crossed overhead, keeping a watch on their leader's dorsal fin. Barkley stared at the over forty-foot megalodon. His gills were as long as Barkley was from snout to tail.

Speaking with Drinnok now seemed like the stupidest idea in the world. Barkley could probably creep away if he was careful, but he shook the thought from his mind. Gray had seen something in the prehistore king and Barkley trusted his friend's judgment. If there was any way to avert a war, he had to try, even if it meant his own life.

That brave thought did not, however, stop his voice from squeaking when he said, "Drinnok, King of Fifth Shiver, I seek an audience."

The king's ears were sharp. With a swish of his giant tail, he spun himself. Drinnok stared at Barkley, who repeated, "Drinnok, King of Fifth Shiver, I seek an audience."

"I heard you the first time," he replied. "I'm trying to figure out what you are, and how in the name of

Tyro you could sneak up less than a tail stroke from my gills."

Barkley dipped his snout low. "It's more like three tail strokes for me, your majesty."

"Yes," Drinnok agreed. "You are very small."

The bull shark that Barkley had evaded earlier rushed over. "My king! Are you all right? Shall I eat the intruder?"

Drinnok flicked his fin at the prehistore bull. "No, Rastor. Now that this puny dweller has evaded every layer of your defenses, I will question him myself."

"But, but King Drinnok—" the bull sputtered.

"Why don't you change the patrol patterns, Rastor?" Drinnok said. "Or should I choose a more competent captain for my guard?"

Rastor dipped his head. Before swimming away, he eyed Barkley in a way that told the dogfish his life was over if Drinnok dismissed him. The megalodon king swung his head, with its giant mouth and dagger teeth, toward Barkley once more. "Your audience is granted. You have two minutes."

"First, is Hokuu here?" Barkley asked, looking around. He didn't see the frilled shark. "If he is, I request that he not be allowed to listen."

"One minute and fifty seconds," Drinnok said.

Better make it good, Barkley thought. "My name is Barkley and I'm here as a representative for Gray, who you know as Graynoldus. He wants you—"

"The pretender who fancies himself the Seazarein?" interrupted Drinnok. "He wants me to do what, exactly?"

Barkley dipped his snout to the gigantic megalodon. "Gray specifically told me not to use the title of Seazarein in front of you. He wants you to know he never desired to be the Seazarein but it was forced upon him when Hokuu sent Kaleth to the Sparkle Blue."

Drinnok grunted. "Another pretender, but a worthier one. Continue."

"Gray doesn't want to go to war with Fifth Shiver," Barkley told the king.

Drinnok interrupted him. "Because he fears me."

Barkley dipped his snout again. "With respect, King Drinnok, Gray isn't afraid of anything. He doesn't want war because he believes that there's room enough in the ocean for all of us."

"Is this another trick?" Drinnok demanded. "The last time your pup wanted to talk, his allies attacked us."

Barkley shook his head from side to side and gave Drinnok an emphatic tail swipe. "Gray was after Hokuu, who has said that you want to send every shark here to the Sparkle Blue. He had to try to stop that, as you would if the situation was reversed. But when Gray saw you, he felt you weren't that type of shark. He even went to the Underwaters to check. He agrees that it's dangerous there and wants everyone who wants to come up to be able to. He knows it was Hokuu behind King Bollagan's death." Barkley gave Drinnok a smile. "If he's wrong, I suppose I'll be eaten right about now, as it's been two minutes. But if he's right, maybe we could speak some more?"

Drinnok nosed Barkley out of the greenie. "What type of fish are you?" he asked.

"I'm a dog shark, your majesty," Barkley answered. "Some call me a dogfish."

"You are entirely tiny. Your teeth are so small you couldn't have sent me to the Sparkle Blue if you had a day to chew on my gills as I slept."

Barkley clicked his mouth shut. He wasn't about to give a smart-alecky answer here. Too many lives were at stake.

"I'm not insulting you, dogfish, but in my home you wouldn't survive a day."

"Are you done not insulting me, your highness?" Barkley asked. "There are pressing matters to discuss."

The big megalodon laughed. "What I mean is that you're a smart and cunning shark, even though you are small. You were able to evade my royal guard. None of my enemies in the Underwaters has ever gotten this close, and many have tried. And what about Takiza? He's even tinier than you, but powerful as a seaquake. Who knows how many seemingly weak sharkkind were sent to the Sparkle Blue because the Underwaters are so dangerous? Perhaps some of them would have had the chance to grow up like you, or Takiza, and discovered skills that would make all of Fifth Shiver stronger."

Barkley was dumbfounded and couldn't answer for a few seconds. "King Drinnok, that's one of the nicest things that anyone has ever said to me. And smart. I can't believe a shark as big as you would realize something like that."

Drinnok cocked his head. "Is that because you think large sharkkind are stupid?"

"No, no," Barkley said. "That's not it."

Drinnok poked Barkley with his immense snout, sending him skidding a good ten feet. "You should laugh when a king makes a joke."

Barkley was petrified. "Ha, ha, ha . . . funny."

"I would speak with young Graynoldus," Drinnok said. "But if this is another trap . . ."

"It's not, your majesty," Barkley said. "He does ask one thing, though."

Drinnok became wary. "And what would that be?"

"Can you keep this a secret from Hokuu?" Barkley asked. "Graynoldus doesn't trust him."

"Hokuu is a powerful ally if there were to be a fight," Drinnok said. "To not bring him might be considered foolish."

Barkley nodded. "True. But Gray is waiting with only a few sharks, not an armada. If your scouts see more, you can always leave. And if it's like I say, you can bring all your mariners to the meeting. That's how badly Gray would like to avoid war."

Drinnok studied him. "You are an interesting shark, Barkley. Very interesting, indeed."

BETRAYED

CHAPTER 18

GRAY NERVOUSLY SWAM BACK AND FORTH AT the meeting area outside the fire waters. When he'd sent Barkley to talk with Drinnok, it seemed like a wise decision. His friend was the only fin who could sneak past everyone and speak to the Fifth Shiver king without enraging him. Sending Takiza or a finja like Shear would have started a war for sure. Barkley was the only choice.

But now that Gray had time to mull it over, it seemed like his worst idea ever.

What if Drinnok simply ate Barkley?

Gray scanned the waters and saw nothing. "What was I thinking?" he muttered.

"It was a good decision," said Shear who swam above him, matching Gray's every move while guarding his dorsal fin. "You are the Seazarein. You cannot—"

"Yes, Shear," Gray said, interrupting the prehistore tiger. "I'm the Seazarein. I can only risk the lives of others and never myself. Blah-de-blah-de-blah-blah."

The finja captain of the guard harrumphed. "You're risking your life right now, attempting to meet with Drinnok without your armada. Foolish."

"The AuzyAuzy mariners are not my armada," Gray answered.

Shear replied, "They are all your mariners should you wish it."

Gray circled up and bumped the tiger from his position. "Well, I do not wish it. And stop hovering over me. It's like swimming under a cloud."

"Oh if only I could guard you by hovering," Shear said. "You swim from side to side like an expectant father. At least let my mariners blend into the waters." Shear gestured toward the finja, silently on guard, but visible, as they were not using their abilities to hide themselves.

"I told you, no. I don't want Drinnok thinking this is a trap."

Gray did stop moving back and forth. Here, Shear was right. Though Gray was nervous, he shouldn't be showing that fact to everyone. It didn't send the right message to Drinnok or even his own mariners. He was the Seazarein, after all.

"He comes," Shear said, again from above his dorsal fin. The tiger had returned to his position over

Gray while he had been thinking. The guardian captain could be very tiring. Gray flicked his fins and snapped his tail to get the blood moving. Drinnok moved forward with five of his Fifth Shiver prehistores, most likely the sharkkind of his Line. The rest hovered fifty tail strokes away, wary and alert.

"Shear, don't do anything unless I order it," Gray told his captain of the guard. "Understood?"

"I hear you," the tiger answered in a clipped tone.

Gray swam out to meet Drinnok—and Barkley!—between the two groups of sharkkind. "Good to see you, Bark," he told the dogfish. He was so relieved his friend was all right that his heart was pounding. He tried not to show this but Drinnok noticed anyway.

"You care for your mariners," Drinnok said. "That is good. Some born into positions of power don't realize that their orders have consequences."

Barkley remained silent, hovering at Drinnok's massive flank. He didn't join the conversation because it was between the two leaders. Barkley also didn't swim over to Gray's side for protection. With Drinnok's prehistores all around, it wasn't as if that would guarantee his safety anyway, and it would be an insult to the king.

Gray nodded. "Every fin and dweller's life has great worth. And I don't like to order anyone to take a risk that I wouldn't face myself."

"Nor should you," Drinnok said. "It's the coward's

way. But this time you were right to send another as I wouldn't have listened to you after our first meeting."

"I didn't order that attack," Gray said.

"Your friend Barkley explained," Drinnok said. "I believe him. He also tells me you remember nothing of your father. Is that true?"

Gray nodded. "It is."

"I knew him well," Drinnok said. "He was a constant urchin spine in my gums." The megalodon king nodded to himself. "But I respected him. Your father didn't care about hurt feelings when he gave advice. He wouldn't say what I, Bollagan, or anyone wanted to hear if it wasn't the truth. That is admirable … most of the time. In other cases, when the decision is very important, a leader must decide and his subjects must obey. Don't you agree?"

Drinnok was a more thoughtful shark than Gray would have imagined. It proved you could never judge a shark by looks or size alone. He was smart and laying a verbal trap here.

"I would say that I'm like my father in that way," Gray answered, choosing his words carefully. "I don't expect Barkley to agree with me on everything. In fact, if a day goes by without him complaining, I'd be worried. I think it's okay for someone who has earned my trust to disagree with me on even the most major of decisions."

"But he had to earn that trust," Drinnok countered. "And you would make the decision that was best for the sharkkind in your shiver even if he didn't agree, would you not?"

Drinnok had Gray there. "I would and have," he told the bigger megalodon.

"Your ally Takiza kept us imprisoned in the Underwaters," the prehistore king stated.

"Because he feared what you might do to us," Gray said. "He thought you had led a coup and betrayed your king, sending everyone in his Line to the Sparkle Blue."

Drinnok slashed his tail through the water so hard it churned up greenie from the seabed. "I would never swim such a low and dark current! I would have challenged Bollagan and fought him snout to snout if I wanted to rule. That is our way and my right. But it would have been dishonorable. Instead, I waited for his final answer."

"But others didn't wait," Gray said. "It wasn't hard for me to find out who killed Bollagan, so you must know also."

Drinnok nodded. "It was Grimkahn. The dwellers in our Underwaters are powerful, not like here. After it had been done, there was nothing to do but swim aside or claim leadership."

"Takiza didn't know that," Gray said. "He didn't know you well enough and couldn't take that chance of not acting. And it wasn't only Grimkahn. Hokuu helped."

"That was his right and choice. Only the strong survive the Underwaters. And you don't know me either," the megalodon king added.

Gray flicked his fins up and down in agreement. "That's true. But you're here now so I can see you're a thoughtful fin. I'd like to think I am, too. I think Fifth Shiver should have the choice whether they want to live here or there. I won't block you from coming up."

"And you'll give up the throne of Fathomir?" Drinnok prodded.

Gray shook his head. "With respect, King Drinnok, I can't. As you say, we don't know each other well, so I can't leave the safety of my friends and family to someone I don't know."

"Then where does that leave us?" Drinnok asked. "I am the king of Fifth Shiver. I was in Bollagan's Line before you were born."

"I have no doubt you proved yourself in the Underwaters and earned that position," Gray told the megalodon. "But in the Big Blue, I've proved myself."

"I grant you that," Drinnok grumbled. "Now that we've met, I see you're not entirely unsuited to lead. But still, I will not dip my snout to you."

"I'm not asking you to. You rule Fifth Shiver— that won't change," Gray told the king. "Perhaps in time you'll lead everyone. Who knows? Until then, we should agree to live in peace. We can all live in peace."

Drinnok nodded. "I believe this is worth trying."

Gray exhaled, relieved. "I'm happy to hear you say that."

"And so am I!" said a familiar voice. Gray and Drinnok turned to see Hokuu. He weaved his eel body, which rippled in excitement. "Because those words will be your doom!"

CHAPTER 19

GRAY TAPPED DRINNOK ON THE FLANK. "WE should swim away right now."

"Swim away?" said Drinnok. "From a frill shark? He answers to me! Your inexperience shows, Graynoldus. Watch and learn."

Barkley bumped Gray. "You're right and I don't like this. Hey, I'm sounding like Shear."

The tiger finja was over Gray's dorsal fin. "Which means you're being smart for once."

Drinnok yelled at Hokuu. "Explain yourself! What are you doing here?"

Hokuu snapped his lithe tail in the water and pointed. "Isn't it obvious? I wanted to see with my own eyes when the king of Fifth Shiver betrayed everyone who swims in the Underwaters."

"You question me?" Drinnok roared. "I am your leader! You follow my orders!"

Hokuu's emerald eyes glittered with hate. "And I have been doing just that, my king," he said. The frilled shark waved his lithe tail with a flourish as a monstrous sea crocodile crested the ridge next to him.

The beast was seventy feet long and as wide as Gray was long. His giant snapping jaws could swallow a school of marlins in one bite.

"Is that—is that . . . a mosasaur?" Barkley asked in awe.

"Grimkahn," Gray whispered.

Drinnok slashed his tail back and forth in anger, sweeping away a section of coral reef. "What's he doing here, Hokuu?"

"You ordered me to free more of your subjects from the Underwaters, so I did," the frilled shark answered.

"You know I meant sharkkind!" Drinnok yelled.

"Of course you did!" Grimkahn interrupted. "That order, like the others that come out of your mouth, was foolish. I won't be led by a fool any longer, Drinnok. None of us will!"

"This is gonna go bad, and fast," Barkley said.

Hokuu swam by the giant mosasaur's side. "The Underwaters have nearly been cleared of your vain sharkkind filth! The dwellers and frill sharks rule there now! As it will be here!"

"Mariners, to me!" Drinnok shouted.

The megalodons formed a giant pyramid formation. It was impressive because of how large each of the prehistores was, but there weren't enough of them. Though Drinnok's forces would have easily beaten Grimkahn—and maybe even Hokuu with him—those two hadn't come alone.

Other mosasaurs appeared, not as large as Grimkahn, but most bigger than Drinnok or his mariners. A swarm of at least a hundred giant frilled sharks joined the megalodons, these all at least twenty feet long. The frills weaved and slithered between the giant jurassic dwellers.

Grimkahn roared, a ferocious sound at once rumbling and screeching. "You will be lunch today, Drinnok. It turns out that the crabs here need to eat, too!"

Hokuu twirled his tail and a glowing orb of energy gathered. "You have insulted us jurassics and frilled sharks for the last time!"

"Attack!" shouted Drinnok, as he launched himself forward.

But at that moment Drinnok was struck by a stream of Hokuu's energy and stopped cold. He drifted from the pyramid formation, sinking. His Line wanted to help him, but Grimkahn and the others came at the megalodons, forcing them to put up a wall to protect their king. All the Fifth Shiver sharkkind were under heavy assault from the jurassics and the frills in seconds.

Gray darted to where Drinnok lay on a reef of

purple coral, away from the battle for now. "We have to help him," he told Barkley and Shear.

"There's no way to move his bulk," Shear said.

Gray whipped his tail through the water. "We have to try! I won't leave him behind."

"He weighs a ton!" Barkley said. "Literally. Way more than that, actually."

"They are right, Graynoldus," Drinnok said in a weak voice. He coughed, gasping for breath, and blood drifted from his nostrils. "You must go."

The megalodon king looked with dying eyes at his mariners in the battle. The Fifth Shiver sharkkind couldn't defend against both the ferocious might of the mosasaurs and the lightning quick attacks of the frilled sharks. Over half of Drinnok's mariners were swimming the Sparkle Blue already. The others would join them shortly.

"I don't want to leave you to them," Gray said.

"My life is forfeit and I refuse to have your blood on my conscience," the mighty king said. "Go. Save your friends. Save the ocean. Do this for me . . . and your father . . ."

And with that King Drinnok of Fifth Shiver died in the Big Blue.

Hokuu watched in satisfaction as the jurassics and frills fed on the remains of Fifth Shiver. A few mosasaurs and more than a few frilled sharks had been sent to the Sparkle Blue, but it was worth it. Drinnok was gone. Gray and Takiza still had to be dealt with but their time would come.

Soon.

Grimkahn swung his massive head from Drinnok's bloody carcass and looked at Hokuu. "You have proven yourself today, frill," he said. "Many have promised you things and never given them to you."

Hokuu dipped his lithe neck to Drinnok as the jurassic leader flippered his bulk from the seabed. "Some fins do not keep their promises." Little did Grimkahn realize how much his own life depended on keeping Hokuu happy. If Hokuu had to teach him the same way as Drinnok, he would. He waited to see if this jurassic had learned the lesson of respecting him.

"Well, not me! I want everyone to hear this!" yelled Grimkahn loudly enough that all the other jurassics and frills stopped eating to listen. "This is a new ocean, a new world, and the dawning of a new age! Fifth Shiver is dead." Grimkahn slapped Drinnok's corpse in the flank with a clawed flipper. "Fifth Shiver is nothing more than this carcass. I will lead you as king of Sixth Shiver. Show me you agree!"

All the jurassics bowed at once. The frills waited until Hokuu dipped his own snout, which he did only slightly, but enough to acknowledge Grimkahn as leader. The rest of the frilled sharks followed, although not as enthusiastically as the jurassics a moment before.

Grimkahn chuckled. "As I thought. You frills are not as excited to serve me."

"We have been betrayed before," Hokuu said. "As you have rightly pointed out."

"Unlike Drinnok, I say what I mean and I mean what I say. You've proved your worth so I would like you, Hokuu, to join my Line . . . as my first."

Hokuu had expected—had planned for this moment—to be asked to the Line, but was prepared for a position of fourth or even fifth. No worry there. He could move up as those ahead of him died. And they would have.

But to be named first in the Line! Above every other jurassic—even every mosasaur! It was an honor. Hokuu almost found himself consumed by real emotion.

Grimkahn went on, "These waters are held by the pitiful descendants of Tyro—the same fins that left our kinds off the First Shiver Line. We owe them nothing. They will either dip their snouts or become food. There will be no peace! We will take what we like whenever we want, for we are Sixth Shiver!" Grimkahn turned back to Hokuu. "So, will you serve me, Hokuu? Will you serve me as my first?"

It was the right current to swim. He would earn the respect of the jurassics. Let Grimkahn lead for now. When the time came, it would be Hokuu who was king! He dipped his head below his entire body and raised it with a genuine smile. "I will!"

And the ocean trembled as the frills and jurassics cheered as one.

CHAPTER 20

GRAY LISTENED AS HIS FRIENDS, NEW AND OLD, put forth their opinions on what course of action would be best to combat the jurassic threat. Striiker was readying the Riptide armada, so he wasn't present. That was just as well. The great white's forceful personality sometimes prevented others from speaking their minds. Besides, there was no two ways about it: Striiker was a fighter; he was needed on the front lines. By now the great white had swum the diamond-head for Riptide longer than Gray. The mariners were used to his booming voice and Gray wasn't about to change things before facing their biggest threat yet.

He wished that Mari was here. He had walled off his emotions but couldn't help noticing that her calming influence was missing from the meeting. Gray could only hope Mari was happy and at peace swimming the Sparkle Blue. Though he tried to squash his feelings into the back of his mind, the consequences of that day would always haunt him. Gray's mind had been shocked with grief, disbelief, and anger after Mari was killed by Hokuu. He was battered and rammed by Shear and his guardians and they had led him back to Fathomir.

That wasn't where they should have gone. It was a mistake.

If Gray had been thinking clearly, he would have swum to AuzyAuzy Shiver and joined with their full armada.

But he hadn't.

Now the two armadas were separated by Grimkahn's forces. It would be suicide for Riptide to fight the frills and the jurassics without AuzyAuzy supporting them. At the same time, they were cut off from the landshark canal that would have let them take a shortcut and get to the Indi Ocean, where they could have met up with Xander's force in the Indi homewaters.

They were trapped in Fathomir with no one to come to their aid.

Gray focused his attention on Onyx as he went through a summary of the scouting reports. Between Barkley, Takiza, Shear, Snork, Leilani, Velenka, and Onyx himself, there was a loud and lively mix of opinions. Judijoan had fallen into the role of designated shusher when someone spoke too much.

Usually one or two shushes were all it took to quiet the offending party.

For now, Gray only listened. He had seen Lochlan, the former king of the Sific and leader of AuzyAuzy Shiver, do the same thing when he was alive. Loch would allow his Line to argue among themselves about the best course of action as he hovered quietly. They would thoroughly exhaust every option, even coming up with ideas that Loch himself hadn't thought of. This process allowed the golden great white to make the best decision.

"So, for now everything is quiet," Onyx said, ending his report. "But the jurassics will be coming sooner rather than later. I recommend we send out hunting parties to stock up on food before this battle starts."

"Like we have a choice," Velenka grumbled.

Snork waggled his bill. "Is there any chance that they won't come? I mean, what makes this spot so special? We can always hope."

Barkley gave the sawfish a pat to his flank. "It's not bad to hope, but that's all it would be."

Onyx nodded. "By the ancient ways, it will be understood whoever rests their fins on the throne in Fathomir has earned the right to be called Seazarein."

"Is that so true, I wonder?" asked Leilani. "It hasn't always been the case, you know."

Gray found the knowledge that the spinner brought to these strategy sessions invaluable. If they survived

Grimkahn, Gray was going to have to figure out a way to keep her as an advisor to the Seazarein. Both Kendra and BenzoBenzo wouldn't like it but he would insist.

Onyx slashed a fin through the water, interrupting Leilani. "If you think that great, toothy jurassic will speed by the golden greenie of Fathomir without so much as stopping in for a hello and good day, then you are sadly mistaken, my pretty young pup."

"Shh!" hissed Judijoan at Onyx. "Don't be rude. Let the lady speak." For some reason Judijoan had taken an instant liking to Leilani, treating the spinner shark as if she were a daughter.

Velenka had noticed this also and didn't like it. "Looks like there's only one lady here, huh? I don't remember you sticking up for me like that," she said to the oarfish.

As much as she liked Leilani, Judijoan disliked Velenka. She gave the mako a quick "Shh!" and motioned for Leilani to continue.

"Um, yeah," the AuzyAuzy shark went on. "What I meant was that Fathomir wasn't always here. There were at least two other places. One was Atlantis—the island, not the sea. That's gone and sank. The other no one is exactly sure where it was, but it did exist. Probably in the Sific somewhere . . ."

"A crackerjack point you've made!" said Onyx. He swished his tail derisively. "Be sure to mention it to Grimkahn as he's swallowing you whole."

Judijoan raised herself perpendicular to the floor, towering over Onyx. "If I have to ask you to be civil once more, I won't be asking. Shear will be bumping your snout from this cavern. Is that understood?"

Onyx looked to Gray on the throne. "We must prepare for the attack that will surely come. It's foolish not to!"

Takiza swished his own gauzy fins back and forth. "Foolishness can come in many forms, Onyx. You would do well to remember that."

The blacktip settled into a sulky hover.

Velenka nodded at Onyx. "Relax, old fin. It wouldn't make a difference, anyway. Grimkahn and Hokuu are coming. One is the strongest dweller that's ever swum in any ocean, the other the best there ever was at shar-kata. Defense is a waste of time."

Gray thought about the truth of this. If it was only Grimkahn and his mosasaurs attacking, they could probably hold them off. But with Hokuu's shar-kata energy blasts roasting anyone who tried to defend a choke point, staying inside Fathomir amounted to a trapped death sentence.

Barkley shook his head at the mako. "Sure, Velenka. Maybe we should all hover outside in a row for them to eat us."

"We'd be less tired when our time comes," she answered.

"Like you'd wait around to swim the Sparkle

Blue," Barkley said. "You'd sneak away as soon as the fighting started."

"Of course I would!" the mako said.

Now Gray did interrupt. He swam off his chair and slashed his tail through the water to keep everyone quiet. "Why would you sneak away?" he asked.

Velenka looked at Gray. "You're going to make me say it?"

"I'm not going to make you do anything," Gray said. "But please, tell me exactly why."

Velenka flexed her fins, embarrassed. "Because the chaos of them going after you would give me my best chance to get away."

Leilani shook her head in concert with Judijoan. "You only look out for yourself," the spinner said. "Disgusting."

Gray swam a quick circle as he met everyone's eyes. "But she's right. Leaving when they were chasing me would give her or anyone else the best chance of getting away. Grimkahn will come after me. He needs me to swim the Sparkle Blue and he wants to be the one to make that happen. And Hokuu wants me gone, too."

Barkley slapped his tail against the rough cavern wall. "Leilani's point is important, sure. It's not Fathomir Grimkahn wants. It's Gray." His friend gestured at him with a fin. "But if you think we're going to let you swim off to be a distraction so we can get away, you're crazy!"

Onyx dipped his snout to Leilani. "I bow before the lady and apologize for my earlier sarcasm. But unless someone can explain how swimming into the open ocean is better than defending the strong point that is Fathomir, I suggest we make do. All things being equal, there's no better option."

Gray nodded at Onyx. "But knowing this does give us the option to leave if we can think up a way to make it unequal and in our favor, which is exactly what I'd like everyone to do."

Velenka rolled her eyes. "Grimkahn and Hokuu are between us and AuzyAuzy, who could already be destroyed to the last fin."

Barkley gnashed his teeth. "I hate when she's right," he said, gesturing at the blacker than black mako. "We can't join up with anyone unless we could somehow fly over the Arktik ice."

"Why fly?" Leilani asked. "You could swim between the icebergs. It wouldn't get you to the Indi Ocean, though. Only the Northern Atlantis."

Gray focused on the AuzyAuzy spinner shark. "Wait, what do you mean? It's winter. Everything's frozen, and it would take months to go around."

Leilani became nervous when she noticed everyone was watching her. "Um, that used to be true twenty and thirty years ago. But it's been warmer for a while now, so not as much ice. The Arktik isn't frozen solid like the old days."

"You mean there's a way through?" Barkley asked. "Now? Today?"

"Sure," answered Leilani. "It's called the Northern Passage. It comes out in the Northern Atlantis by the Spine at the end of the Tuna Run. Is that important?"

It certainly was. Their discussion lasted long into the night.

CHAPTER 21

GRAY SWAM OUTSIDE THE THRONE CAVERN IN the Fathomir homewaters as Striiker left to prepare the Riptide armada. Judijoan was outstanding at scheduling his meetings so that sharkkind and dwellers arrived exactly as he needed. Gray couldn't bear lying on the throne inside the mountain strong point and came outside because he needed a change of scenery.

Takiza and Snork had already been dispatched on a secret mission. Gray had asked the betta if the sawfish was ready for such an important role in their plan. Takiza had replied, "He is as ready as you were when I sent you for the maredsoo before the Battle of Riptide."

That didn't give Gray a boost of confidence.

When Takiza had ordered Gray into the depths of the Dark Blue to retrieve the glowing energy greenie called maredsoo, he didn't know why it was important.

If he hadn't succeeded in that mission, their forces would have been defeated in the Battle of Riptide by Finnivus. If that pressure had been added to Gray's already plentiful nervousness and fear, he would have failed for sure. But Takiza would keep what they were actually doing from Snork, just as he had with Gray. The betta had called for another ally to join them also. All Gray had gotten was that his name was Salamanca and that he was a blue marlin. Takiza refused to say anything more about him.

Gray was past getting mad about the betta keeping secrets. Let his old master do what he thought best. He was a good and goodly fish and Gray trusted him. Besides, as the Seazarein, Gray had many other currents to set in motion.

He saw Judijoan waiting for his signal to send over Shear. Gray nodded and the captain of his guard swam over.

"Seazarein," the guardian finja said, coming to attention hover before dipping his snout.

"Could you stop that, Shear?" Gray asked.

"I am greeting the Seazarein as that position commands," he said. "You can let your friends bump your flank or slap your belly, but I refuse."

"What if I ordered you to tail-slap my belly?" Gray said.

"Since I have spent many days swimming by your side, I'd know that you were joking." While Shear's rigid ways could sometimes be annoying, they also could lighten Gray's mood from time to time.

As the tiger always reminded him, Gray was the Seazarein. "What if I politely asked you to shimmy around in a victory swim to lighten my mood because it would help me make an important decision that might save lives?"

This caught Shear by surprise. He had to think a bit. "Before doing my victory shimmy, I would have to report to Takiza and the rest of your friends that you might be mentally unstable and so unfit to make any important choices." He dipped his snout to Gray. "I would, of course, only be doing that for the good of those same fins who you had hoped to save by making me shimmy about like a fool."

"Good one, Shear," Gray said. "Okay, fun's over. I'd like you to send three of your mariners to the Stingeroo Supper Club. Have them talk about how we're preparing to escape using the Northern Passage in the Arktik. Tell them not to be overheard, but they must have the conversation there."

Shear looked at Gray, his face unreadable. After a moment he asked, "Is this a joke like the victory shimmy?"

"No, Shear," Gray told him. "I want Grimkahn to follow us, so I need Trank to know. But they can't say it like they want him to know it. Your mariners need to take all precautions to not be overheard."

"But how will we know that the stonefish has heard? What if my mariners are too good at preventing anyone from hearing them?"

"Because I trust in Trank's deviousness." Gray gave Shear a tail slap to the belly. The big tiger stared balefully and then swam off.

After Shear left, the colorful flying fish quickfin zipped to a stop in front of Gray. He flared out his four wings and snapped them downward in a salute. "Quickfin Eugene with a message from Xander del Hav'aii, second in the Line of AuzyAuzy, currently residing at Indi Shiver in the Indi Ocean guarding Tydal, minister prime of Indi Shiver. Code word: Red Tang. The message is as follows—"

"Wait," Gray said, and the flying fish stopped speaking and went into attention hover. He wasn't immobile like a shark, though. He kept the same position by madly vibrating his wings so fast it caused a buzzing noise in the water. This was kind of funny and Gray struggled not to laugh. "I thought your name was Speedmeister?"

"It should be 'cause I'm so fast," answered the flying fish. "But the oarfish—your advisor, Judijoan, I mean—she said to use my given name here."

Gray looked over at Judijoan who was smiling and talking with Leilani. She did take time to point at the flying fish sternly with her tail, though.

"What's Xander's message?" Gray asked.

"The message is as follows. 'Tydal's getting the hang of things. We can meet at the Tuna Run if needed.' That is all." The flying fish waited for a reply.

Interesting.

Gray had discounted Xander being able to help them as he was so busy keeping Tydal alive and Indi Shiver from plunging into civil war. But if Xander could peel off a hundred of his fastest mariners, he might be able to meet them in the Atlantis. In theory.

Gray decided it was worth a try. "Tell Xander to bring whatever mariners he feels can safely come away from guarding Tydal. The swim back will take you a day, right? You'll have to avoid our enemies, you know. Maybe use that flying trick where you go above the chop-chop."

"Yes, Seazarein Graynoldus," answered Eugene. "I won't get caught."

"Make sure he gets the message and leaves as soon as possible."

The young flying fish snapped to attention once more and recited the Quickfin Oath:

> Through brightest ocean and down
> darkest lava tube,
> in calm water or heavy seas,
> no whorl current,
> nor flashnboomer, nor iceberg'd
> waters,

no dead zones, nor exploding fire
waters,
no seaquake, feeding frenzy, or even
landshark nets
shall prevent a quickfin from deliver-
ing their message
on time and anywhere in the Big Blue.

Eugene bowed once more and asked, "Is there anything else, your lordship?"

"Tell Judijoan that I order her to call you
Speedmeister," Gray said with a smile.

"Oh, please don't make me do that, Seazarein
Graynoldus," Eugene said, his face losing some of its
color. "She scares me."

"Yeah. Me too," he told the quickfin. "On your way
then, Speedmeister." The flying fish beamed when Gray
used his nickname. He gave one last four-winged salute
and then flashed away with a high-pitched buzz.

Leilani came over when Eugene had left and
dipped her snout.

"Not you, too," Gray told the spinner.

"I can't salute as fancily as"—Leilani checked
that Judijoan wasn't watching before saying—
"Speedmeister does it, but I do want to show respect,
Seazarein Graynoldus."

"I get enough respect, Leilani," he told her. "Please,
call me Gray."

Leilani flicked her fins up and down. "Okay, Gray. So, do you have a mission for me?"

"For you?" he asked.

There must have been too much surprise in his voice and the spinner's eyes narrowed. "You don't have to be so astounded. Even though I don't have too much experience, I can do things."

"I know you can," Gray said. "You've already been a great help. Having you around is like having the complete history of the Big Blue swimming alongside me." Leilani didn't know how to react here and waited for him to continue. "Which is a good thing!" he added.

"Okay..." she answered. "Judijoan sent me over to tell you it's time for you eat."

"Lunch already?" Gray asked.

Leilani smiled. "Dinner actually. The sun's about to set. Well, not set, but travel to another part of the Big Blue."

"Dinner," Gray said to himself. It seemed like moments ago he had come out of the throne cavern. The day had completely gotten away from him. He became worried.

Grimkahn probably wasn't wasting any time.

"None of the scouts have reported anything," Leilani said, reading his mind. "But this might be your last meal for a while, so make it count." The spinner turned to leave.

"Leilani," Gray called. "Do you want to hunt together, maybe?"

The spinner shark smiled. "Sure," she answered. "I'd like that."

SALAMANCA

CHAPTER 22

"I'M FREEZING," SNORK SAID TO TAKIZA AS HE chopped stalk after stalk of tough brown-greenie. Here in the North Atlantis where the water was colder and the currents faster, the greenie was harder to chop through.

"Ah, a complaint. I thought perhaps you were the first apprentice who would not do that," Takiza said from his position above Snork. "False hope, indeed."

Snork watched as the betta moved his gauzy fins this way and that, using his shar-kata skill. The chopped greenie rose upward and joined the other stalks that had been cut in an overhead mass that didn't move, even though there was a current that should have pushed it. With all that was going on in the Big Blue, Snork had no idea why he was here cutting down greenie, and Takiza wouldn't tell him anything. All they seemed to be doing was making a great big mess.

"Does that mean I'm your apprentice?" Snork asked.

"Oh no," said Takiza, shaking his head and whipping his tail through the water for added emphasis. "It is too soon for me to take on another Nulo. Please understand, it is not you. It is me. Gray's infinite number of questions combined with a knack for not listening to instruction tired me so greatly that I cannot at this time be anyone's Shiro." Takiza looked at Snork, who was panting from the effort of chopping over two hundred stalks of greenie. "Tell me, Snork, have I become forgetful in my old age?" he asked.

"I—I don't know," Snork answered. "Why do you think that?"

"Because you have stopped cutting stalks of greenie," Takiza said. "And I do not remember saying the words that would tell you to do such a thing. Have I?"

"No, Takiza," Snork answered. He began chopping stalks of greenie once more. The betta fluttered his fins and the brown-greenie gathered in the water above them. "My bill hurts a little."

"Of course your bill hurts!" said a giant of a marlin as he neatly blocked Snork from striking a thick stalk of greenie with his own longer and thicker bill. "You swing it in an exceptionally *estúpido* manner! As if you had only woken just this morning with it attached to your face!"

The magnificent marlin was the biggest Snork had ever seen. He was cobalt blue on his upper half and silvery white on the bottom, so shiny that he glittered in the sunlight. His upper jaw was elongated and formed a majestic—and sharp—bill that made up at least four feet of his eighteen-foot length. He also had two flashy hooks in one side of his mouth. Though it couldn't be possible, the hooks seemed to be in the perfect spot to be a decoration! Would a swordfish do that on purpose? It was too much to believe.

Takiza gestured with a fin. "May I introduce Diego Benedicto Pacifico Salamanca. It is he who will be teaching you how to be a bladefish."

"I can see that Salamanca is sorely needed here," the marlin said. He tapped Snork on the head with his bill before butting him to the side with his tail. He spoke rapidly and with an accent. "A bladefish must strike when his fins are level, the tail slightly angled in the opposite direction, countering the force of your blow, and your eyes—your eyes!—they must always be fixed on the point of contact—nowhere else! Now, *observar*!"

The marlin chopped ten stalks of greenie. He went left and right, left and right, and sliced through each of them with no effort whatsoever. The greenie even landed in a neat pile, stacked onto itself.

It was amazing.

The swordfish turned to Takiza. "Why would you

181

teach him this, this, this—horrible form? Did you want to bloody his nose? Or were you teaching the *estúpido* manner first so he would know what not to do?"

Takiza rolled his eyes at Salamanca and said, "I did it this way because teaching him to fly was even less productive."

"You can fly now?" the billfish asked. "Salamanca would see this."

Takiza sighed. "Stop your annoying games. You are intelligent enough to know that since I do not have a bill, I cannot instruct him in the correct way for a bladefish apprentice to strike a blow."

Salamanca nodded. "That is sadly true. Your nose is pitiful in its lack of length. Certainly not the nose of a bladefish, although you do have many other good qualities." He tapped Snork's head once more. "What's your name, boy?"

"Snork."

"Snork? Snork, you say." Salamanca proceeded to emphasize his name in different ways. "Snork. Snork. Snooork. Hmm." The marlin looked him over. "Are you fond of this name?"

"Well," Snork said. "It is my name."

"It is not the name of a great bladefish," the marlin said. "And if Salamanca trains you, you will be a great bladefish. When Salamanca does incredible and amazing things, the fins and dwellers who are fortunate enough to have witnessed them say things like, 'The incredible and amazing Salamanca was just here,' or 'Your life is now meaningless as you have missed the fantastic feats the incredible and amazing Salamanca has just performed.' I am unsure if a fin named Snork can do incredible and amazing things."

"Think of it as a challenge," Takiza said. "Or are you afraid of a challenge?"

"Salamanca fears no fin, dweller, landshark"— at this point the marlin showed off the hooks in his mouth to Takiza which caused the betta to roll his eyes—"or challenge." Salamanca looked Snork over, using his bill to poke, prod, and tap his flanks, dorsal, tail, and stomach. "Did you know the landsharks prize catching a blue marlin such as myself above all other fins? They try to do this with a stick and thin rope they call a rod and reel. Though I have given them a chance to ensnare me, none are able. A marlin over one thousand of their pounds is named a grander. By their measure, I'm a three grander, certainly the most grand of them all."

"Are you through being ridiculous?" asked Takiza.

"My process cannot be rushed," Salamanca said. "If I make a commitment, I'm bound by honor to see it through." He tapped Snork on the head again. "Where do you hail from? Perhaps your Line comes from the waters of España, where most great bladefish are born?

"No, not there," he answered. "I'm from the North Atlantis."

"Cold there," said the marlin. "It doesn't suit me. Takiza tells me your father was a bladefish, but you did not know this."

Snork agreed. "He never said a word."

"Ah, interesting," Salamanca said, thinking to himself. "A humble practitioner of the art of bill-kata. Tell me, what was his name?"

"Uprush."

"He was called Uprush and then named you Snork?" Salamanca waved his bill from side to side. "I do not think I like your father."

"It was my mother's favorite name and you take that back!" Snork said, his temper flaring. His father was swimming the Sparkle Blue. No one should be speaking that way about him.

"I will not," Salamanca said. "And further, I think he did a bad job raising you." The marlin slapped Snork on both sides of his face so that it stung. "What do you think of that, boy?"

Snork had been taught by his mother and father to never fight when someone called him names. When you were a sawfish, it wasn't like being a regular shark; bumping or ramming could hurt or even kill someone. But after being slapped, and having his father's memory insulted, Snork forgot everything and rushed at Salamanca's flank trying to skewer him. The huge marlin swerved to the side and faced off with him, bill to bill.

"En garde, Snork!" The marlin hacked at his head in a downward strike. Snork had allowed the taps before, but now blocked as his father had taught him. Salamanca then struck left, then right, left twice more, before coming from the right again. It was almost too fast, but Snork managed to deflect each blow.

"Say you're sorry or you'll be sorry!" Snork yelled.

"Never!" Salamanca exclaimed. "What will you do now?"

Snork rushed at Salamanca. It was crazy and dumb. The marlin was easily three times his size but Snork was so mad he didn't care. He faked at Salamanca's head but spun in the water to poke at his gills, and then attempted a strike to the marlin's flank. Through it all, Salamanca never got mad. He deflected Snork's bill each time, moving and weaving in the water, always just out of reach. "He is muy bueno," the marlin said over his shoulder to Takiza.

Snork stopped. "You're doing this on purpose. It's a test," he sniffled. Realizing this didn't make him feel any better, though.

Salamanca dipped his bill in the water. "But of course. And I apologize for insulting your undoubtedly noble father—he was a bladefish and we are all noble, every one—but I needed to see the extent of your training, young Snork. You would never have tried your hardest if you didn't lose your temper."

"I told you the boy has promise," Takiza said.

"*Si, si.* Salamanca will do this. Soon fins and dwellers will be saying, 'Look at the great and amazing things that Salamanca's apprentice the mighty Snork can do!'"

"I am overjoyed," Takiza told him. "Can we begin his training?"

"*Si,* I know you are eager for this. Exactly how would you like to proceed?"

Takiza bowed with a flourish. "As you have said, my nose is sadly short, but I think you should show your new apprentice how to chop down this entire field of greenie."

"And there is no way for you to help in this?" Salamanca asked the betta. Snork thought the question was curious but remained quiet.

Takiza motioned upward with a fin. All the greenie that Snork had chopped down earlier hovered against the current, eerily motionless. "I cannot," he said. "I am an old fish who can only do one thing at a time."

Snork looked out over the field and his heart sank. It was immense! He had been cutting down greenie for hours and Salamanca's test had made him even more tired. There was no way they could chop the entire thing down. It went on for miles!

The marlin saw the look in Snork's eyes and gave him a light tap to the flank. "Two bladefish working together can do anything!" he exclaimed. "Remember that, o' mighty Snork. Now come, we begin. Watch until you understand how to cut properly, then join me."

"I already know how to chop greenie," Snork said.

Salamanca shook his head up and down, and then side to side. "You do, but you don't."

Snork was going to swim forward as soon as the marlin began cutting but ended up watching for a full ten minutes as Takiza floated above them both. The reason Snork observed for so long was that he kept noticing the tiny adjustments that Salamanca was making. It seemed so easy: chop a stalk and move forward to cut the next. But the way the marlin did this simple thing was so elegant and precise that Snork could only hover in awe.

Salamanca brought his head to the side just so, his tail counter-angled in the other direction. By the time the marlin's bill struck the greenie, his tail had moved so it was in a straight line with his bill. As Salamanca followed through the stroke, his tail went the other way the exact same distance, completing half a tail stroke. This forward motion from the half tail stroke brought Salamanca forward to the next stalk. The follow through from the previous strike had his bill in position for another, but now from the opposite direction. In this way the marlin managed to cut down a stalk of greenie every single time he moved his head left or right, and all the while he was constantly moving forward because of his tail's counterstrokes. Not a fin flick was wasted.

It was so graceful that Snork's mouth hung open as he watched. Finally he said, "I don't know if I can do it."

"So you see! *Excelente!*" Salamanca said, not stopping his cutting. "Now that you see how to cut properly, the only way to learn the correct form is by doing it. Today is the first day of your journey to becoming a bladefish as your father before you. But you must join me."

So Snork swam over next to the big blue marlin and tried as best he could to imitate all the little things he was doing. It was hard, and more than a little frustrating. But every once in a while Snork got both his head and tail in perfect position and it was marvelous. When this happened, he didn't even feel his bill slice through the greenie. Then Snork did it three times in a row and that earned a nod from Salamanca, which pleased him to no end.

It was still difficult after that, but also gratifying. And through it all, Snork thought he could feel his father smiling at him from the Sparkle Blue.

CHAPTER 23

AFTER A WHORL CURRENT OF PREPARATIONS, Gray made his will as Seazarein known to everyone else. They would swim through the Arktik into the Atlantis and meet up with Xander at the Tuna Run. He had gotten word that Grinder and Hammer Shiver had already left and only took with them thirty sharks. That wouldn't be enough to do anything except send them to the Sparkle Blue so Gray didn't send for them. It was also too late for Hammer mariners to reach the Tuna Run from their homewaters.

He hoped the AuzyAuzy mariners stationed at Indi that could be spared would come join them, but they wouldn't be too many. The final number would depend on the situation in the Indi homewaters. If the intrigue had settled, perhaps there would be another hundred battle-tested sharkkind added to Riptide's numbers.

They had been swimming for twelve hours in the cold waters of the Arktik and the ice was getting thicker above them. Leilani was sure that the recent warmer temperatures had kept the short cut through the Arktik open. At least that was what the reports of a month ago had said.

But if those reports were wrong, Gray's forces would be walled in, and Grimkahn would catch them.

The jurassics and frills had gotten on their trail far faster than he would have liked. Just as he had planned, Trank had told Hokuu they were heading this way to save his own skin, just as Gray thought he would. His plan had worked too well, though. Gray had to order everyone to increase their speed. Fortunately, Grimkahn's forces had not been seen for several hours now because of the faster pace.

Their group was swimming past areas Gray had never heard of: the Bering Strait, the Chukchi and Beaufort Seas, and now the Northern Passage past the Canada landmass toward the North Atlantis. If Riptide could meet up at the Atlantis Spine with Xander and his AuzyAuzy mariners, they would have a chance to overwhelm Grimkahn with numbers. If not, they would be slaughtered.

They'd left Fathomir soon after a quickfin came with a message from Kendra. Jaunt and the AuzyAuzy mariners had tried to engage the jurassics to slow them down, but the prehistores didn't stop. They roared through the fire waters and then past the AuzyAuzy homewaters. Grimkahn was heard ordering them to keep moving to Fathomir where he would eat the Seazarein's still beating heart.

That's me, Gray thought as he swam, keeping up the twenty-five tail stroke per minute pace that had been set. It was a punishing tempo and only the fine conditioning of the three hundred Riptide mariners allowed them to keep it. Gray hadn't let Striiker bring all their mariners. He left two hundred to protect the Riptide shiver sharks—pups and the moms and dads who needed to care for them, including Gray's mom Sandy and his brother and sister Riprap and Ebbie— along with half the ghostfins inside the golden greenie fields by Fathomir. That was where everyone hid as Grimkahn and his forces swam by.

Now he wished that they had brought more sharkkind.

Gray glanced at Barkley, who led the remaining ghostfins on a fast swim where they formed in a line from tail to snout, but very close together. He gave Gray a fins-up but had to concentrate on keeping his position in the formation.

"How are you doing?" Gray asked Leilani, who was next to him.

She looked a little out of breath, her gills rapidly flicking open and closed. "I'm okay. Since we're limited on how much we get out for long swims, the Eyes and Ears have regular fitness classes to stay in shape." She wheezed, dropping back two tail strokes before catching up again. "I haven't been going as much as I should have."

"Shear," Gray said, moving upward a little and poking the prehistore tiger in the stomach to get his attention. "How about you?"

"I'm fine." Shear was swimming right over Gray's dorsal again. Instead of being a nuisance, it now felt comfortable. "And if you would simply speak, I can hear you," the tiger said. "Kindly do not poke me in the belly."

"Right, right," Gray said. "Sorry."

There would be fighting soon and Gray was used to having a battle dolphin over his dorsal. This time, Olph the battle dolph was swimming near the chop-chop with his brothers and sisters. While dolphins could hold their breath for long periods of time, they couldn't do it forever. Battle dolphs had a system for keeping an eye on things while they moved as a pack near the surface of the water, jumping and leaping through the chop-chop. If there was trouble, Olph would take his position with Striiker to relay his commands in click-razz, which penetrated the waters better than the loudest shout.

He moved to poke Shear's underbelly again. The captain of the guardians adjusted his position and landed a stinging smack on Gray's flank.

"Hey!" Gray exclaimed. "You slapped me!"

"Did I?" Shear asked. "I'm sure I was swimming a course where that shouldn't happen. Unless you were moving up for some foolish reason." Leilani snorted and Gray had to smile. For a shark with not too much of a sense of humor, Shear could be as sarcastic as Barkley when he wanted.

"Any word from the scouts?" Gray asked the prehistore tiger.

"If there is something you need to know, I'll tell you at once," Shear replied.

Gray swam out from under Shear and rolled so he could look at the tiger. "See, when you say it like that, it makes me think you're keeping things from me."

"I would never," Shear answered, turning so he could look at Gray eye to eye. "The guardians do what is best for the Seazarein and you are the Seazarein. Now let me do what I'm supposed to be doing." Shear turned himself and went on swimming as if this proved his point beyond all doubt.

Gray knew that Shear took his job seriously and put tons of pressure on himself since Kaleth was slain. At that same time, Hokuu had devastated the guardian force with his diabolical trap in the fire waters. There were fewer than twenty now. Only twelve including Shear were fit enough to make the trip. The finja guardians, being prehistores and stronger than any of the scouts in the Riptide forces, were tasked as the long-range scouts. Eight were swimming in a loose circle about a mile away; the other four were closer, a thousand tail strokes from each side of the moving formation.

"Ice field ahead! We'll have to descend five hundred feet," Shear said as he looked toward Leilani. "Are you sure this lane goes through?"

"Um, well the information—"

Shear added a slash to his powerful tail strokes, cutting Leilani off. "So you're not sure."

"I knew the risk when I made the decision, Shear," Gray said.

"Wait, he's right. I'm not sure," the spinner answered. "But I do believe it or I wouldn't have said anything."

Shear nodded. That was good enough for him.

Striiker swam out from the diamondhead in their formation and joined them. "Is anyone else freezing their tailfin off? Who in their right mind would live in a place like this?"

"That's another reason to go through this way," Gray said. "The prehistores come from a place that is at least as warm as the South Sific in the summer. They won't be used to this cold."

Striiker nodded. "Probably right. I hate it here and I'm from the Atlantis. They'll be miserable. Ha! Suck freezing algae, Grimkahn!"

Their laughter at this was cut off by a tremendous

CRAAAACK! that thundered through the waters and seemed to go on and on. Everyone instinctively slowed.

"What in the name of Tyro is that?" yelled Shear. It was hard to hear anything.

"Oh no," said Leilani. "I didn't count on this!"

"What?" asked Striiker as a series of screeches, pops, and thundering noises vibrated the entire ocean. "Spit it out!" The big great white used a series of tail signals to order the armada to slow.

"The same warm temperature that kept the path open in the last few years also makes the ice mass unstable! A huge chunk fell into the water!" Leilani told them.

"There are many large pieces of ice in these waters," said Shear.

"It's too loud to be just another piece," she said, looking around the waters. "There! Look!" She pointed with her fin.

Gray and everyone else could see a gigantic piece of the ice canyon, larger than any floating chunk that he had ever seen, descending into the water as it fell. The huge block of glacier was the size of an island. Gray wouldn't have been surprised to learn that a thousand landsharks were living on it. It was heading with the current straight at the thinnest place on their course.

"If that iceberg hits both sides of the passageway we'll be trapped!" Leilani yelled.

"Swim!" Gray ordered. "We have to get ahead of it!"

Striiker rejoined his formation and roared, "Increase speed to fifty tail strokes per minute! Execute!"

This was bad. Very bad.

The armada could keep that pace for maybe five minutes.

Unfortunately, because of the distance they needed to cover, it looked like they needed six.

CHAPTER 24

THE JAGGED MOUNTAIN OF ICE SUBMERGED FOR a moment, then bobbed to the surface like any other iceberg. But this one was gigantic. Free from its place on the canyon wall the current took hold of the ice and pushed it toward the choke point faster than Gray would have believed.

"The Riptide mariners won't make it!" Shear yelled.

Gray saw that his tiger captain was right. He, Leilani, and a few guardians were leading the Riptide formation by ten tail strokes and it didn't look like they would get through either. Only Barkley and his ghostfins, fast-swimming in what they called the sea snake formation, seemed as if they had enough speed.

Olph the dolph had taken his place above Striiker's dorsal and clicked out the pace to the mariners so they would stay in formation while maintaining their pace. The *click-clack*, *click-clack*, *click-clack* that the armada timed their tail strokes to was quicker than Gray was used to hearing. But they still weren't going fast enough to beat the free-floating mountain of ice to the thin part of the passage.

"STRIIKER!" Gray yelled as loudly as he could. The great white's eyes locked onto him from the diamondhead. "MORE!" was all Gray could shout as he increased his own pace. There was a pause, probably not more than a second, when he worried that Striiker had not understood.

Gray didn't know if he had the breath to keep swimming and shout again but then Striiker bellowed, "ONE HUNDRED!"

Olph and his dolphin mates synchronized themselves. Within one tail stroke the speedy *click-clack*, *click-clack*, *click-clack* became an unreal *clik-clikclikclikclikclikclikclik!* There was no speaking while moving this fast. Gray's heart hammered in his chest. His entire body was on fire and it felt like a sharp piece of coral was being pressed through each flank. It was all he could do to suck water into his gills fast enough to breathe.

The floating mountain turned ponderously in the water as the current pushed it. This revealed that the iceberg wasn't circular, but more of a shard. Gray could see that there would be one more turn before the ice would smash into both sides of the passage.

The armada would have one chance. The next time the iceberg showed them its thinner end they might get by on the right. If they didn't Gray and everyone else would probably be ground to paste between the jagged ice and the cliffs on their right side.

Gray risked a peek at Leilani. She was keeping up somehow. And Shear was in position over his dorsal. He wondered if the guardian was laboring at all. Gray couldn't hear anything except the pounding of his own blood inside his head.

The ice mountain was five hundred tail strokes ahead of them. Two hundred strokes in front of that were the cliffs of the passageway. The ice revolved a quarter turn and now the path was totally blocked. If the current didn't push the iceberg around the armada would smash their snouts right into it.

Stop thinking negatively, Gray thought. The ice will move!

The armada was barely ten strokes behind Gray, Leilani, and Shear. They roared toward the iceberg as the *clikclikclikclikclikclikclikclik!* of the dolphs vibrated through Gray's body.

Three hundred tail strokes behind the ice. *Clik-clikclikclikclikclikclikclik!*

Then two hundred. *Clikclikclikclikclikclikclikclik!*

The iceberg was in no rush to rotate. The wide side stayed in front of their snouts.

They were one hundred tail strokes from it. Worse,

the current had pushed the iceberg to within one hundred tail strokes of the passageway's choke point.

Seventy tail strokes away. *Clikclikclikclikclikclik-clikclik!*

Then fifty.

Gray saw a sliver of a blue as the iceberg spun toward its thinner side.

But it wasn't enough for everyone! There was barely room for Leilani and him.

Thirty tail strokes. *Clikclikclikclikclikclikclikclik!*

Finally the iceberg showed them its thin end. There was two hundred feet between the right wall of the passage and the ice.

The iceberg was just fifteen tail strokes from the left side of the passage.

Clikclikclikclikclikclikclikclik!

Gray passed through the gap with Leilani and Shear. He couldn't stop to look but he heard Striiker—who somehow still had enough breath—shout, "MAKE IT! MAKE IT! MAKE IT!"

Clikclikclikclikclikclikclikclik!

Gray felt more than heard the Riptide armada's frenzied tail strokes reflecting off the side of the cliff and the iceberg as they squeezed through just before the wider end came around and pulverized the other side of the passage.

The iceberg groaned and buckled.

The current slackened from the blockage.

Everyone slowed and then stopped, moving only enough to not sink.

"They—they don't—get much . . . closer . . . than that." Striiker wheezed.

"If they do," gasped Leilani, "I'm staying home next time."

The iceberg continued to grind as pressure from current built up.

Barkley came over. He and the ghostfins weren't in their formation and all sucked water into their gills greedily. The dogfish gave Striiker a grin. "What took you guys so long?"

"Shut—cod—hole," managed the great white.

Gray watched as the iceberg was slowly ground to pieces. The passage wouldn't be blocked for long. "We have to keep moving," he said to everyone. "I know you're hurting. I am, too. But we have to make the most of this lead time before the jurassics and frills can get through."

"You heard . . . the Seazarein!" yelled Striiker, recovering his breath. "Quit lazing around like . . . a sunny day on the reef. You know the drill! Fins up and at the ready in five minutes!"

There was a groan but the mariners did it. They were soon on their way once more.

CHAPTER 25

SNORK'S CONCENTRATION WAS SO DEEP HE WAS lost in the task at hand. It was peaceful with the current whisking past and the constant *snik-snak* noise his left and right cuts made. For some reason when he struck to the right it always made a *snik* sound, but a leftward slice was a decided *snak*. When Snork strung together a number of perfect strikes, it went *snik-snak-snik-snak-snik-snak-snik-snak* and lulled him into a relaxed alertness where he could sense the current bending every greenie stalk around him.

It was wonderful.

With a flick of his serrated bill, Snork severed a stalk of very thick brown-greenie. Before Snork began this task he definitely would have had a problem with it. But after studying Salamanca's perfect form it was easy. The last time they had stopped was hours ago. Was it hours? Or days? Takiza had given Snork a piece of maredsoo greenie the last time they had stopped and he lost track of time after that.

The odd kelp made his body fiery hot for a while, but then it had settled into a feeling of refreshing vigor. If Snork hadn't been cutting through a field of greenie before eating the maredsoo, he would have certainly chosen to do it after.

Snork wasn't as good with his bill as Salamanca, but that was to be expected. The big blue marlin had a lifetime of experience and training. Snork had settled into a rhythm, though: chop left, move forward, chop right, move forward, left, forward, right, forward— over and over until it became as natural as breathing. *Snik-snak, snik-snak, snik-snak* the stalks fell as Snork moved through them.

Then there were no more in front of him.

This broke his concentration. Snork looked around.

The entire field had been trimmed. He was done.

He was also alone.

Where did everyone go? Snork thought.

"Hello?" he said out loud.

"I told you he had potential," Takiza said from above.

Snork looked up and saw Salamanca nodding, waving his bill up and down as the sun caught the glittering landshark hooks and fancy lures hanging from the side of his mouth. "This one, he can be *especial*," the marlin told Takiza. He looked down at Snork. "Toward the end, your form was *perfecto*. Bravo!" Salamanca dipped his bill in respect.

Snork watched as the last few greenie stalks he had cut through drifted upward. They rose past Takiza and Salamanca to join the others . . .

"Wow," Snork whispered in awe. The greenie formed into an immense ball of kelp that hovered above them. It would have engulfed the entire Speakers Rock area in the old Riptide homewaters. It was that big.

"Yes," Salamanca agreed as he also glanced at what they had done. "It's impressive what our short-nosed friend can do."

Takiza didn't allow any of the kelp to drift but it did turn and tumble within the boundaries of an invisible bubble that he was creating with his shar-kata power. Other things moved by or through this underwater cloud of kelp: first a mass of red plankton, then a double drove of mackerel, and after that thousands of jellies. These were the deep sea kind of jelly with stubby tentacles instead of tendrils and they flashed light as they drifted into the mass.

The way the jelly drifters flickered their lumo lights, it seemed they were frightened by the eerie sight of the ball of greenie rotating in the moonglow but stubbornly refusing to move with the current. Snork felt the same way. He was more amazed than afraid, though.

"Now that you have this, what are you going to do with it?" asked Salamanca about the greenie.

Takiza flicked his tail at the marlin. "Be quiet for a moment and I will tell you." The betta stared into the distance. Gray said when Takiza did this he was using his senses to check on things far, far away. After a minute he turned to Salamanca and said, "Why, I will let it drift, of course."

The invisible boundary hemming in the greenie opened for a moment and some of the kelp was swept down the towering mountainside that formed the southern part of the Atlantis spine.

"That's it?" asked Salamanca.

Takiza shook his fins crossly. "Of course that is not it! Do you think I would call you if it was only for this?"

"Salamanca does not know!" The marlin became a bit embarrassed and added, "You haven't spoken with Salamanca as much as in the past."

"Because I respect your time!" Takiza said as he released another blob of greenie. That too was caught by the current and spread over a large distance, rolling and tumbling with the current down the mountainside. "I do not want to take you away from your important business."

"Granted, thank you," Salamanca said. "But you could send a quickfin every so often just to say hello." Takiza gave the marlin a flat stare. "It is quite insensitive to not hear from you, whom Salamanca considers a friend."

Takiza sighed. "I apologize if I hurt your feelings."

"*Gracias.*"

The betta gestured after the drifting greenie. "Now, if we could attend to the matter at hand."

"What is the matter at hand?" asked Snork.

Both Takiza and Salamanca turned. "Are you tired, o' mighty Snork?" asked the marlin. "Can you continue? Though we swim with the current, it is a bit of a journey."

"You should not bring him," Takiza said. "It will be dangerous."

The marlin shook his long bill from side to side. "Nonsense! A bladefish receives nourishment from danger! How do you expect him to grow courageous and strong if he receives no nourishment?" Salamanca flicked his tail at him for confirmation. "Isn't that right, o' mighty Snork?"

"Um . . . yes?"

Takiza released another burst of kelp from the ball of greenie. "Make sure he doesn't get himself sent to the Sparkle Blue the very day he has become useful."

"Sparkle Blue?" Snork asked with a start. "Where are we going?"

"Why, where else would Takiza Jaelynn Betta vam Delacrest Waveland ka Boom Boom, the great bladefish Diego Benedicto Pacifico Salamanca, and

the mighty Snork go?" The marlin sliced his bill
through the water in an intricate pattern. "To save the
day, of course!"

CHAPTER 26

HOKUU BURNED THROUGH HIS STOLEN LIFE force energy at a furious rate. He should have had enough dark-kata strength from draining his mako finja to give him superpowers, even compared to his normal shar-kata mastery, for the next fifty years. But creating a passageway between the oceans for Drinnok—what a waste of time that had turned out to be—and then making another hole large enough for Grimkahn and his jurassics to escape the Underwaters had taken up half his stores.

His remaining power was quickly being depleted by two tasks: speeding the currents to catch Gray and his pitiful forces, and keeping the jurassics from freezing to death in the waters of the Arktik and North Atlantis.

Of the two uses, warming the waters was definitely most draining. There was no chance the mosasaurs would have survived the icy waters without him. Hokuu had even seen fear on Grimkahn's face as the giant icebergs rolled and crashed in the unforgiving seas around them. He himself was a frilled shark and could stand the cold (and pressure) of the Dark Blue, so he was unaffected. But the frills with them were born in the Underwaters. They were used to the warmer temperatures there and also had to be protected.

Hokuu wouldn't take any chances with his frilled shark brothers and sisters. After all, he might need them, or their life force, later. But he still felt a pang of bitterness as his powers were used up. He craved more dark-kata! He wanted to be filled to bursting with its force!

His own Shiro had forbidden him to ever use dark-kata, thinking it evil.

He definitely shouldn't have told Hokuu how to do it, then.

Life force energy was so much richer than what you could coax and beg from the oceans. But Grimkahn was adamant and so Hokuu had to use his precious stores of dark-kata to catch Gray. He wanted to eat the Seazarein's heart. The jurassic king's purpose was splendidly single-minded in this way, and Hokuu was happy for this.

They were almost past the Canadian landmass and nearing the Atlantis Spine where the Tuna Run was every year. In fact, it should be happening in the next week or so. Perhaps Hokuu would go with Grimkahn and the rest of the frills and jurassics to celebrate their victory.

Gray's own finja guardians had sealed his fate when they spoke too freely about where they were going at a place called the Stingeroo Supper Club. Hokuu knew about the urchin kings and their network of meeting places. He had even used a few of their assassins on occasion.

It had been easy enough to threaten the manager, Trank, for the information he needed when they found no one at Fathomir. Then it was easier still to follow them. If the fat pup thought Hokuu and Grimkahn wouldn't track their puny forces because the water was cold, he was wrong! And the delay caused by a large iceberg blocking their way for a moment was nothing much.

Still, Hokuu felt a prickle of nerves. The pup had been lucky before. Then there was Takiza to be concerned with. Well, not concerned, but cautious. It wouldn't do to fight the betta without a plentiful supply of dark-kata energy.

Hokuu made a decision and stopped heating the waters. If the jurassics and frilled sharks couldn't take the colder temperatures of these waters then the dream of ruling the Big Blue, aside from the warmer seas in the Sific, Indi, and Caribbi, would be dashed.

Besides, I shouldn't waste my lovely power, he thought.

The temperatures around Grimkahn and his forces dived but Hokuu kept pushing the current to keep the bulky jurassics moving. They would never catch Gray and his sharkkind in the open waters if he didn't.

"What are you doing?" Grimkahn yelled from the position next to him. The jurassic king had insisted that he be at least even with Hokuu as they traveled. "Why did it get so cold?"

"I can't spare the energy to warm the water while going this fast," Hokuu answered with some edge to his voice. He was angrier than he realized about having used so much of his delicious power. Grimkahn snapped his jaws in displeasure but didn't say anything more.

Suddenly a prehistore materialized out of nowhere, speeding straight at Hokuu!

It was a finja guardian!

Hokuu didn't have time to put up a shield as the giant hammerhead bore down on him. But Grimkahn's mighty jaws snapped down on the thirty-foot shark's trunk and shattered its spine. He sawed through the hammerhead's body with his long mouth. Its head and tail broke off and were swept behind them, and Grimkahn swallowed the mouthful that remained.

"That was their rear guard!" Grimkahn shouted to

his mariners, the current taking his words to them. "We are close to Sixth Shiver's first victory!"

There was a cheer from the mosasaurs and frilled sharks. Grimkahn looked over at Hokuu and growled. "If you won't keep us warm then speed up!"

"Grimkahn," Hokuu said, "it would be a harsh drain on my powers. I won't be able to help you in the fight."

"I don't need anyone's help in battle," Grimkahn answered. "Speed us there! I command you!"

Hokuu pushed the current faster. Now he was using even more of his precious dark-kata energy! The life force of the makos would be gone by the time they caught up with Gray.

It was no matter. He could still beat the pup and little Taki with his regular powers.

Once Gray and his Nulo were out of the way, Hokuu could gather more dark-kata power, and he would answer to no one but himself.

But not yet.

He gnashed his sets of tri-tipped teeth together and drove their group forward.

"Back in a few," Gray told Leilani. He did a rolling loop from their position at the front of the armada and slid to the rear with Shear following him the whole way. Gray knew it was pointless telling the tiger finja to stay put so didn't even try. He had to get a look at Grimkahn and Hokuu with his own eyes to see where they were.

The news wasn't good. They were far closer than he would have imagined.

Gray looked at Shear. "You didn't think to mention they were in sight?"

"They aren't a threat yet. You have enough to think about," Shear remarked. "But the ice didn't slow them too much."

Gray had had to make quick decisions before and didn't shy from this one. "We're not going to make the meeting point before they catch us. We need to find a spot where we can only be attacked from one direction."

Shear nodded. "There's an area up ahead that may meet our needs."

And it did! There was a plateau with an outcropping of rock that blocked the current blasting down the Spine. The rock formation prevented the large ledge behind it from being worn away like the rest of the mountainside. And the space was clear of other, innocent shivers, which was a bit odd as this was the time near Tuna Run, but very welcome. They weren't going to find a better place than this.

"Striiker! Barkley!" Gray yelled, getting their attention. "Change of plans!" He motioned with his tail toward the area. They signaled with a fin waggle that they understood.

Gray turned to Shear and asked, "Why do you think no one has taken this spot—" but before he could finish his thought, Gray was pushed twenty tail strokes to the left by a terrifically strong rip current. Both he and Shear struggled to get to the ledge and safety.

"My guess would be that current," Shear answered when they were on the ledge and behind the outcropping of rock a hundred yards ahead of them that checked the vicious current.

The tiger was right. There was no way a shiver could safely fish the Tuna Run without some being swept away and into the rocks of the Spine.

But Gray and his friends weren't here to fill their bellies. They were here to fight.

Thankfully, Striiker saw what happened to them and brought the Riptide armada in from a better angle, as did Barkley with his ghostfins.

"It's perfect," Gray said, as Leilani, Barkley, and Velenka joined him.

"Perfect for what?" Velenka asked. "For Hokuu to roast us alive? Or for Grimkahn to eat our still-beating hearts?"

Barkley gave her a slap to the flank. "Try to be optimistic," he told her.

"Okay. Our deaths will probably be quick," she answered.

Gray ignored the mako and told Shear, "Send your

fastest finja to find Xander and his force and bring them here." Shear dipped his snout and went.

Striiker joined them, careful to avoid the edge of the plateau and its sucking current. "The armada is fins up. Anything comes at us snout to snout, we're gonna have a good chance at shoving them into that rip current no matter how big they are."

"What do you want me to do?" asked Barkley. "Should we join the armada?" The dogfish glanced at his ten ghostfins.

Striiker shook his head. "Don't need you and yours, doggie. You'll only foul us up."

It seemed as if Barkley and Striiker were going to argue, but Gray told his friend, "He's right, Bark. Get down into the greenie underneath the current." There was a much smaller area a few hundred feet down where a few dozen sharkkind could hide.

Velenka was overjoyed. "What a great idea!" she said. "It may be the best idea ever! All hail the great and wise Seazarein!"

Sometimes the mako could be unbelievable.

Barkley shook his head. "Gray, we didn't swim all this way to hide while you fight. At least, Leilani and I didn't."

"What's wrong with hiding?" asked Velenka. "It's smart. By the way, you shouldn't be disagreeing with the Seazarein."

"Would you get a hold of yourself?" Leilani told

her. Velenka scraped her needle teeth together in anger but shut her mouth with a glare. The spinner looked at Gray. "We can help."

"I know," Gray said, nodding. "I'm counting on that. Grimkahn will come at us with brute force. But I don't think Hokuu will."

"I see," Barkley said. "We put our noses in the greenie and wait for a shot at his belly."

"Exactly," Gray told Barkley and Leilani. "If you see a chance, strike. But watch yourselves and stay safe." After a moment he added, "You too, Velenka." The mako was surprised. She nodded and followed Barkley and Leilani off the plateau exactly as Shear came back.

"I've sent half my remaining finja to find Xander," he told them. "But I can't be sure if he even got our message."

"I'm confident the quickfin got through," Gray said, thinking of Eugene Speedmeister.

Shear nodded. "Even so, I cannot promise anyone will arrive in time to help."

Striiker came over and gave Gray a scrape on the flank. "Just the way I like it," Striiker said, giving Shear a bump, too. "I don't want any latecomers sucking up our glory when we snout-bang this Grimkahn flipper back into whatever stinking hole he swam up from."

Shear thought about this and then, lightning fast, gave both Gray and Striiker a flank slap with his tail.

"Let us do this thing, then," the big tiger agreed.

"That's what I'm talkin' about! Riptide, are you ready?" Striiker yelled. The three hundred sharkkind snapped to attention hover in perfect time. "Yeah, they're ready to rumble," Striiker said.

It was then the first greenie stalks tumbled into the area.

THE BATTLE OF THE SPINE

CHAPTER 27

"THERE THEY ARE!" CRIED HOKUU AS HE stopped pushing the current under Grimkahn and his forces with his dark-kata powers. He was more tired than he would have liked, but no matter. They numbered over a hundred jurassics and frills. Riptide had barely three hundred fins total, the majority of them regular sharks, not prehistores.

What a delightful massacre! Hokuu thought.

"At last!" cried Grimkahn. "The cowards will plead for death for making me chase them all this way!" He released a screeching roar, and the other jurassics and frilled sharks shook off their weariness and locked eyes on their king. Grimkahn gestured with his flipper at the plateau-ledge where Gray's pitifully small armada hovered. "No survivors! And leave the Seazarein to me!"

They were less than a quarter mile from the pup and his mariners when the Riptide sharkkind suddenly disappeared!

What happened?

Then Hokuu saw. A mass of floating kelp had drifted into an eddy in front of their position. This was odd, but not unheard of.

Still ...

"Grimkahn!" Hokuu said. "The greenie blocks our view!"

"So what?" the mosasaur spat. "There isn't enough to hide from me!"

"Perhaps we should be careful—"

Grimkahn roared, the sound hurting Hokuu's ears and stopping him mid-sentence. "When I want your opinion I'll command you to speak! Otherwise, shut up and attack!" With another terrible shrieking cry Grimkahn dived toward his prey with the rest of his mosasaurs and frills close behind.

Hokuu slowed as more and more greenie gathered in front of the plateau where the Riptide mariners hovered. There was no reason to be in the first group, after all.

Gray willed the greenie stalks swirling a hundred feet in front of him to increase in number. He breathed a sigh of relief when he saw the first ones. The kelp wasn't being carried away by the current. It was gathering up into a large globe.

That most likely meant Takiza was here.

They had a chance if that was the case. There was still so much that needed to fall into place, though. And the timing would have to be perfect. Could Takiza do his part? Gray couldn't worry about that. The ancient Siamese fighting fish didn't need anyone to do that. Besides, Gray had bigger things with which to concern himself.

Grimkahn and his jurassics, for example. The mosasaurs were immense.

Some were as big as a fully grown blue whale. Any of them could swallow a mariner whole. Riptide couldn't afford to let even one of the monsters onto their small plateau. If they had to fight the giants snout to snout without the advantage of the rip current, every Riptide shark would surely swim the Sparkle Blue.

Shear and Striiker watched the mosasaurs and frilled sharks drive fearlessly into the far end of the thick greenie. They would be through in less than a minute.

"Protect the Seazarein!" shouted Shear to the six finja prehistores hovering around Gray.

"Forget that!" Gray said. "Make sure none of Grimkahn's forces get onto this ledge!" He turned to Striiker and gave a fin signal.

"Riptide armada, divide battle fins into double clusters!" ordered the great white. The command was clicked out by the battle dolphs over the rush of the current and the increasing rustle of the swirling greenie. Everything would hinge on keeping their position, so each battle fin of a hundred now separated into groups of twenty. Instead of the entire armada acting as a single formation, groups of twenty sharkkind would attack any jurassic or frill that managed to make it to the ledge.

Striiker turned to his mariners and yelled over the noise. "Very soon a bunch of flippers are coming to try to eat us! You remember Hokuu? I sure do! It's him that we're fighting! He may come in different shapes and sizes, but it's the same filthy worm that destroyed our homes!" Striiker shouted as loudly as he could, "RIPTIDE MARINERS! WE ARE GOING TO WIN THIS BATTLE! WE WILL HOLD THIS LEDGE UNTIL EVERY STINKING MONSTER IS DEAD OR GRAY SAYS DIFFERENT! DO YOU GET ME?"

"WE GET YOU, SIR!" the Riptide mariners roared.

"They come," said Shear to Gray.

The first through the greenie were the frilled sharks. The eel-like creatures didn't look fast but that was an illusion. They were lightning quick. They didn't blast out of the greenie so much as squirt from between the stalks forming the globe.

"DOUBLE CLUSTERS AT THE READY!" Striiker shouted.

The initial wave of frills didn't roar straight at them. They tried to juke and jitter as Gray had seen Hokuu do in battle. It was hard for a defender to stay in position to defend when a frilled shark could shift to either side and strike at a flank.

But these attackers were fooled by the calm waters within the greenie. Since it wasn't moving fast why would the water thirty feet away by the ledge be any different?

Mistake.

The wicked current took the frills totally by surprise. Two of the first five were folded in half, their flexible spines not flexible enough to withstand the pressure. The other three were mashed into each other. They were swept into the rocks, which crushed their skulls and scraped the skin from their bodies when they hit the jagged mountainside.

If only all the frills and jurassics had attacked together; then maybe the battle would have been over. But that wasn't the case. Grimkahn's forces moved in a loose pack so only the first and fastest swam the Sparkle Blue. The other frills recognized the trap and stopped.

Being slower, the mosasaurs did not see this. Two pushed the frill sharks in front of them into the current, and so ten more frilled sharkkind were swept into the rocks. The first giant mosasaur, at least ten feet larger than Gray, wasn't strong enough to withstand the current. In a stroke of luck, he was the furthest up the current. When he tumbled, he took several other jurassics with him!

For a fleeting moment Gray felt a surge of hope.

They would hold the ledge.

They could not only win but maybe wouldn't lose a mariner!

That thought ended when Grimkahn blasted through the greenie a split second afterward. Yes, the mosasaur leader was surprised by the current, but he was so terrifically strong he overcame it.

Grimkahn smashed into the ledge and used his gigantic jaws to battle the lower part of the Riptide formation. He sunk the huge claws on his flippers into the rock and would not be moved. "TO ME!" he shouted. "TO ME!"

Two other mosasaurs made it the ledge, holding fast with their own clawed flippers.

"DOUBLE CLUSTERS; ONE, TWO, AND THREE!" shouted Striiker. "GO, GO, GO!"

Blocks of twenty sharks launched themselves at each one of the mosasaurs. They struck the jurassics in the face and ripped at their flippers. One monster tumbled away, but Grimkahn and his ally crunched sharkkind bodies in their terrible jaws, throwing the broken bodies of Gray's mariners into the current.

Other frills found a way to avoid the worst of the current and joined the fight. They were smaller but still twice as long as most of the sharkkind defenders. Striiker kept sending sharks to ram those that attempted to gain the ledge.

"FOUR, FIVE, SIX, SEVEN! GO! GO! GO! GO!" he yelled.

But for every frilled shark rammed back into the current, another made it onto the ledge. Once free from that obstacle, the frills were deadly. They jittered side to side, using their spiked tails to stab sharks through the gills and eyes. Gray saw one mariner die from a tail spike though the skull before he swam over and bit down on that attacker's head.

Grimkahn yelled at Gray, "Today you die, Seazarein! You will all die!"

"You must get to safety!" shouted Shear to Gray. "We must retreat!"

"No!" Gray answered. "We're staying!"

Hokuu remained five feet inside the greenie so that he was unseen as he slithered through it. He could feel that the kelp was being kept in a circular bubble by shar-kata energy.

Takiza was near.

But where?

Hokuu watched as Grimkahn fought snout to snout with Gray's mariners. The much smaller sharkkind were doing a good job protecting their position. Still, they were slowly losing ground. If Grimkahn got his entire body onto the plateau it would be over. Without the current threatening to rip the jurassic from the mountainside, Gray would be lunch.

Hokuu saw the pup Seazarein save the life of the captain of his guardians, a sickeningly loyal tiger finja named Shear. Hokuu began to weave his dark-kata power into a bolt that would send both to the Sparkle Blue. This would be detected by Takiza, so Hokuu would have to speed to a different position afterward, but the risk was well worth the reward.

Hokuu released his ball of orange energy, and it zipped straight at Gray and Shear.

But the current got hold of it.

The globe of crackling power detonated inside a group of twenty sharkkind and vaporized them. Their blackened remains were sucked away by the current. Hokuu cursed himself. He should have corrected for the rip current! If those twenty sharkkind had been with the whole Riptide formation the energy would have leapt into every mariner! All would have swum the Sparkle Blue instead of a mere twenty!

Once again he couldn't believe Gray's luck.

Hokuu thought he felt someone coming his way from underneath. He couldn't see through the whirling greenie all around him, but that didn't mean someone wasn't there. He zipped away, changing directions several times. Hokuu would make his way forward to try again.

And this time my aim will be true, he thought.

"You did that on purpose!" Barkley hissed at Velenka as the frilled shark zipped away. "Hokuu must have seen you."

The mako shook her head. "If he spotted us we would be dead. Especially me."

"I don't think he saw us, Barkley," Leilani said.

The three of them could see only bits and pieces of the fight going on by the ledge above them because of all the tumbling kelp. Their position ten feet underneath the mass allowed them a clear area to view inside and sometimes through the greenie as they hid in the short and thick scrub kelp below.

They had spotted Hokuu after he released an orange ball of energy and it lit up the waters. Barkley didn't see who or what was hit. He hoped Gray and everyone else was all right. If they had just been able to spot Hokuu a little earlier they could have attacked his belly.

"We should try to find him," Barkley said.

"Track a frilled shark in that mess? You can count me out!" Velenka exclaimed, a little louder than she should have. Even though the current and rustling greenie were loud it was never wise to give your position away.

Leilani flicked her fins in disgust. "I guess we can count you out of everything!"

"I wish you would!" the mako replied.

"Quiet," Barkley told her.

She slashed her tail through the water. "I won't! This is crazy!"

A frilled shark rose behind Velenka. It wasn't as large as Hokuu, but that didn't make it any less terrifying. Its red eyes glowed as it reared back and opened its mouth, filled with deadly, tri-hooked teeth.

"LOOK OUT!" yelled Barkley as he streaked forward and butted Velenka straight into the frill's stomach. The prehistore's gaping mouth crashed into the rock bed behind them, a flipper length from taking Velenka's head off. "SWIM!" Barkley shouted, and they both broke in different directions. The frilled shark was disoriented from driving his face into the stony seabed and lost Barkley and Velenka.

But Leilani was hovering a foot above the scrub greenie and directly in front of the beast. It locked its crimson eyes on her and whooshed forward. Barkley knew there was no way for him to defend the spinner shark.

Leilani was about to die when . . .

Something happened.

Not something, but someone.

Snork.

The sawfish rushed underneath Leilani and bolted

upward as the monstrous frilled shark reared back to send her to the Sparkle Blue. This time, instead of striking with his mouth, the monster sent his spiked tail through the water so fast it made a high-pitched whine.

Snork whipped his bill from right to left and smashed the monster's tail into the ground! It must have hurt because the frilled shark let out a howl. Barkley blinked, sure he was dreaming. The enraged prehistore roared and tried to bite Snork's head off. But the sawfish never stopped moving and whipped his bill in the other direction. It met the enraged frilled shark's neck and cut its head off!

Swimming over to the speechless Leilani, Barkley asked Snork, "How—how did you do that?"

"I don't know," Snork stammered. "I've been practicing, though."

They all stared at the frilled shark's head slowly spinning in the water in front of them. It had a look of absolute surprise frozen on its face, probably the same one that Snork and Leilani were wearing.

"I'll say you have," Barkley told the sawfish.

Just then the sounds of the battle above increased once more.

CHAPTER 28

THE BATTLE HAD TURNED INTO A FEROCIOUS melee. Gray roared forward and rammed a frilled shark in the gills. He didn't stop swimming until he pushed it off the ledge and it was swept away. Three other frills had managed to make it onto their defensive position. Striiker sent mariners to fight the beasts, but the Riptide sharks were no match for them.

"Re-form around the Seazarein!" Shear ordered the remaining finja guardians.

"No!" Gray yelled. "Have them attack the frilled sharks!"

"You need to be protected!" Shear shouted.

"We're all going to die if Grimkahn and his jurassics take this position!" Gray answered. "Striiker can't concentrate on the jurassics if the frills are behind him! Now do it!"

The guardians were technically Gray's to

command but they did look to Shear, who was responsible for the Seazarein's safety. He gave them the signal to go. "Clear the area. Then resume guarding the Seazarein."

"Let's take out that mosasaur!" Gray told Shear as he gestured to the one farthest from Grimkahn.

"You're making it very hard to protect you!" the tiger finja said, but he streaked with Gray at the jurassic that had gotten onto their plateau. Grimkahn and another were making progress, but the Riptide mariners' attacks were keeping them off balance. Twice they had dislodged one of their taloned flippers, but each time Grimkahn and the other mosasaur found another spot on the mountainside to sink their claws into and hold fast.

The opening to the ledge was smaller than the back part, where the Riptide mariners were arranged. This was good, as it created a choke point. Only three of the giant mosasaurs could try to get onto the area at once. The current above and below the outcropping was too strong for someone to swim against with someone defending.

"We have to get that one off!" Gray shouted over the sounds of battle. "I'll get its attention, you bang it on the head!" He didn't wait for Shear to respond. Gray swam under the mosasaur's jaw and gave it a tremendous fin slap. The jurassic roared as broken teeth rained from its mouth. When the mosasaur stretched forward to snap at Gray, Shear rammed it in the skull.

The jurassic tottered as the vicious current tugged at its tail. But it didn't fall away. And Gray and Shear were out of room. Striiker and the remaining Riptide mariners couldn't aid them. They were all fighting.

"GOLDEN RUSH, ATTACK!" cried a voice.

At that moment Xander came swimming down from above them. The AuzyAuzy mariners numbered only a hundred. A single battle fin was all that could come down from the mountainside and onto the plateau at once. They bashed into the mosasaur attacking Gray and Shear and blew it clean off the ledge. Once the current hit the monster it was swept away and struck the mountainside solidly.

The AuzyAuzy mariners bit and chewed at the newest mosasaur until it couldn't hold on any longer. It too was carried off by the rip current.

"Sorry we're late," said Xander. "It was a bit of a scrumble to get here."

"By my thinking you're right on time!" Gray said, giving the hammerhead a quick flank bump.

"Yes, right on time! To die with your friends!" roared Grimkahn as he got his fourth clawed flipper up on the plateau. He was out of the current. "Now you'll pay for defying me!"

Within moments he and his other mosasaur mariner were both on the plateau. Other jurassics grabbed for the ledge behind their leader. Striiker's forces had been pushed out of position and couldn't do anything about it.

Hokuu crept close to the edge of the greenie mass, being careful not to expose himself. It looked like Grimkahn had finally gotten the upper fin—or, in his case, flipper. He and his forces were going to wipe out the pup and everyone else. Sure, reinforcements had come, but only a single battlefin of a hundred mariners. That wasn't enough. Not nearly.

Hokuu grinned as he took it all in. There was nothing that could stop Grimkahn's rise to absolute power.

And with that, my own, Hokuu thought.

He reveled in the chaos unfolding in front of his eyes, loving every second of it.

This beautiful interlude was interrupted by a faraway whale call. It was distorted, coming from a great distance with the raging current. Hokuu tried to block out the noise but it nagged at the back of his mind. The whale call sounded again, intruding on the moment of his victory once more. Then a group of bluefin tuna flashed by, sparkling as the sun reflected off their silvered bodies. It was a small group. They were propelled by the fierce current and so were gone in an instant.

Another group flashed by, this one twice as large.

Then Hokuu realized what was bothering him.

The Tuna Run! It wasn't happening this week...

It was happening now!

Hokuu realized that they had blundered into a devious trap. He understood the great danger that was coming for Grimkahn, the jurassics, the frilled sharks, and most importantly for his own hopes and dreams.

He darted forward, intent on getting to the safety of the ledge and warning Grimkahn.

Hokuu braced himself to swim through the current but was pulled back into the kelp ball by some force. He found himself looking at Takiza, who hovered in the chaotic mass of greenie as if it were the calmest of days in the Caribbi Sea.

"Leaving so soon, Hokuu?" the betta asked. "I thought you and I might speak."

"You thought wrong!" Hokuu spat. "But I can stay around long enough to kill you!"

He brought his power to bear and shot a bolt of electricity at Takiza. It was blocked easily, as Hokuu knew it would be. He had only done it to get close enough to launch what he liked to call *hurling grace*, his vomit attack. The acid in his stomach was thick and stuck to whatever it hit, dissolving anything covered within a minute.

But the betta was too quick, zipping away and stinging him with a shock to the flank. "Your puny powers alone can't beat me!" Hokuu shot his spiked tail through the water.

It would split Takiza in two—

But his attack was blocked and pushed wide!

A huge marlin then smacked him on the forehead with his bill, causing Hokuu's eyes to water and vision to blur for a moment. "My name is Diego Benedicto Pacifico Salamanca, and I am here to take your measure."

"Salamanca," Hokuu said in disgust. He knew of the billfish and didn't like him one bit. "I thought you never left the waters of Spain and Portuga."

"It was a nice day for a swim," the marlin answered. "Now, I would see you fight. En garde!"

Hokuu was enraged. He forgot about Takiza and fired his tail at the disrespectful blue marlin. This buffoon didn't even have brains enough to be afraid for his life. Well, Hokuu would teach him fear right before killing him!

As a target, Salamanca was too large to miss. But the bladefish blocked each one of his tail spike attacks, clanging them off his stout nose.

"You are as unskilled with your tail as you are ugly," the marlin said.

What am I doing? Hokuu thought. Why am I fighting this fool snout to snout? He was Hokuu, master of shar-kata! He whirled his tail, gathering power.

But a searing charge of electricity sent by Takiza disrupted his concentration.

The betta waved a gauzy fin in a scolding manner. "Using your powers against a foe without his own would be less than honorable."

Then, instead of running, Salamanca closed the distance between them. Hokuu tried gathering energy for a quicker shar-kata attack, but he was again jolted by Takiza.

"Fine!" he yelled at the marlin. "I'll send you to the Sparkle Blue the old-fashioned way!"

"*Excelente!*" the crazy marlin answered. "It is for this Salamanca has come!"

Hokuu fought with the marlin on a purely physical level. He would kill Takiza's friend right in front of him. But Salamanca blocked and parried his strikes. The billfish was incredibly agile over short distances. Hokuu used every tail attack he could think of: over the shoulder, from underneath, around each side. Feinting one way, attacking the other.

Nothing worked.

Then Salamanca jabbed his sharp bill right inside Hokuu's nostril!

Pain exploded inside his head and all Hokuu could smell was his own blood. The marlin shook his bill and said, "You are deeply disappointing."

Luckily for Hokuu the marlin had to dodge when a drove of bluefin ripped through the greenie. These were the fastest tuna, leading the way for the others. Soon the main mass of fish would come through and demolish everything in their path.

Hokuu made the only decision he could.

He fled.

Grimkahn would find out about the Tuna Run soon enough.

Striiker sent wave after wave of mariners at Grimkahn and the five mosasaurs that were marching forward on the ledge. Riptide and AuzyAuzy mariners fought bravely. Some were crushed by the terrible jaws of the jurassics. Frilled sharks also took lives, but Shear and his guardians were using their finja abilities and scoring mortal hits to their gills.

"Dip your snout into the muck and call me king!" yelled Grimkahn. "I'll make your trip to the Sparkle Blue a quick one!"

"Thanks, but no thanks," Gray told the giant jurassic. "Xander, it's time!"

The scalloped hammerhead nodded and gave a tail waggle that was seen by the rest of his mariners still at the top of the Atlantis Spine. They had been warned about the current after the first wave and corrected for it as they dived down the rockside.

Grimkahn swung his giant tail through the water and cleared his area of an assault team headed by

Striiker himself. "It is only a matter of time before I have you in my jaws!" he told Gray.

"That's right, Grimkahn! It is only a matter of time!" Gray said as he saw the stream of bluefin off to the side thicken. The Tuna Run would whip past in barely a minute. "And yours is up!"

"BREAK, BREAK, BREAK!" bellowed Striiker.

Olph clicked out the command but the area was small enough that the great white's shout did most of the work. The Riptide mariners, along with one AuzyAuzy battle fin, scattered to make room for wave after wave of new mariners. A full three battle fins of AuzyAuzy mariners came at the mosasaurs and pummeled them to the edge of the ledge.

Gray was about to lead the charge to finish them with Striiker but Xander put his tail out. "Hold on for a bit," he said. "I've got a surprise for you, savvy?"

Then two Indi Shiver battle fins streaked into the fray, led by Tydal!

"For Indi Shiver and VICTORY!" Tydal shouted.

These were the superbly trained remnants of the Black Wave armada. Each battle fin twisted and turned on their way down, confusing Grimkahn and the jurassics to no end. The mosasaurs took the combined impact of the battle fins straight to their face and trunks. The giants were ejected from the plateau's ledge right as the main body of bluefin tuna came through.

Gray's forces had timed it perfectly.

The main body of the Tuna Run roared through the area like an unstoppable force.

The mariners on the ledge cheered as the frilled sharks were destroyed by the speeding tuna, each weighing five or six hundred pounds and all traveling so fast they were a silvery blur. The mosasaurs were bludgeoned and swept away.

Grimkahn hung on the longest, his flippered claws tearing out chunks of the mountainside as he was hammered by the bluefin smashing into his side. "YOU HAVEN'T WON!" he shrieked. "THIS ISN'T OVER!"

"It is for today!" Gray answered, and then he rammed Grimkahn between his eyes.

The great mosasaur finally lost his grip and tumbled away with the current.

They were safe.

For now.

CHAPTER 29

GRAY AND THE WEARY SHARKS FROM RIPTIDE, AuzyAuzy, and Indi Shivers got back to the Indi homewaters a week later. Gray insisted on only moving as fast as their wounded mariners could swim. No one would be left behind to make it on their own.

Gray looked around the private meeting cavern in the Indi homewaters. Shear hovered at his side, of course. Barkley, Leilani, Striiker, Xander, and Tydal chatted among themselves while they waited. On the other side of the room was the very odd trio of Takiza, Snork, and a large blue marlin called Salamanca. Velenka had been missing since a frilled shark had attacked her, Barkley, Leilani, and Snork at the Tuna Run.

No great loss there, he thought.

Gray also had to answer several quickfin messages that had found him at Indi. This was an unwelcome new development. Apparently, messages and the problems contained within them could find him even if he wasn't in the throne cavern in Fathomir. He waved at the First Court Shark, Oopret, who was an epaulette shark like Tydal, to send another messenger in.

"Seazarein," Oopret said, bowing. "The last quickfin."

"Thank you," Gray told him. "You've done a fine job organizing them." The epaulette beamed and dipped his snout all the way to the rock floor before sending in Eugene Speedmeister.

Gray couldn't help but grin as the young flying fish zipped in. He stopped and flicked his four wings downward in a snappy salute.

"Quickfin Speedmeister with a message from Kendra, regent of AuzyAuzy Shiver in Prince Lochlan's name, code word Whorl Current. The message is as follows. 'Jurassic and frills spotted in Sific. Grimkahn and Hokuu are with them.' That is the end of the message."

The room went silent as everyone, even the overly loud Salamanca, stopped speaking. Gray flicked his tail to the quickfin. "Wait for my reply outside. Oh, and Speedmeister, I'd like to request that you be assigned to Fathomir as one of my permanent messengers. Would that be okay with you?"

Eugene saluted once more before leaving the

cavern, his eyes brimming with tears of joy. "That would be just fine, your lordship."

"I suppose having either Grimkahn or Hokuu out of the way was too much to hope for," Barkley said.

Salamanca whipped his bill through the water. "If Salamanca had one more moment he would have put paid to Takiza's mortal enemy, Hokuu."

Takiza ruffled his fins. "The Tuna Run giveth, but it also taketh away."

"What will you do about Grimkahn?" asked Leilani.

"The short answer is, I need to stop him," Gray said. "Negotiations won't work. We're going to have to win."

Tydal flicked his tail from side to side as he thought it over. "If I were him, I'd look for reinforcements. Another passage to the Underwaters, perhaps?"

Gray nodded. The epaulette had a keen mind, and it was worth considering what he said. "They were spotted by Kendra's fins. They probably aren't there just because the water's warm."

"We should definitely stop that," Xander said. "Wouldn't want to fight an armada of jurassics, now would we?"

Gray looked at Tydal. "How's everything here?" he asked.

The epaulette understood what he meant. "Thanks to Xander, all right." Tydal gave the AuzyAuzy commander a flick of his fins. "Things have calmed."

Gray nodded. Without Tydal's additional help they might have lost. The epaulette could be a tremendous ally in the future. Gray had an idea on how to set that current into motion.

"It only took banishing one of the royal families, and the rest fell straight into line," added Xander. "You think I can maybe go home, Gray?"

Gray shook his head sadly. "Sorry, I need you here to help Tydal train another three battle fins of Indi mariners."

Tydal swished his tail. "With our recent history that's a rather large force for us to have, don't you think?"

"You have control of this shiver," Gray answered. "I need you as an ally, not someone whose homewaters we're occupying."

"But after the Black Wave . . ."

Gray shook his head. "This isn't going to be the Black Wave. I want a combined Indi and AuzyAuzy peace force that will guard this area until the threat is over."

Xander nodded. "Okay, I'm game. I can see how that's pretty important."

Striiker added, "Not knowing where they're going to strike next, it's very important."

"Agreed," said Shear.

"Besides, this place got much less boring once Tydal put the royals in their place." The hammerhead gave the epaulette a grin. "Maybe Indi Shiver is the place for me for now."

Tydal dipped his snout in thanks. "I'm very happy to have you, Xander."

Salamanca slashed his bill through the water, getting Gray's attention. "Seazarein Graynoldus. May Salamanca borrow your friend Snork for a while?"

Takiza gave Gray a fin flick that indicated he agreed. "It would be good for him."

"Right, like lifting rocks good, huh?"

Takiza gave Gray a haughty look. Salamanca had asked earlier if the sawfish could go and learn the ways of their bladefish society. But in the end it was Snork's decision to make. Gray turned to the sawfish and asked, "Is that what you'd like?"

Snork nodded. "I think it's the current I should swim."

"Good. Any other business, then?" Gray asked.

No one said anything, and he was about to end the official audience when First Court Shark Oopret poked his snout inside the cavern. "I beg your pardon, Seazarein. A mako named Velenka would like to speak to you."

Gray motioned for her to be sent in. There were varied reactions around the room.

"The bad clamshell returns," Barkley muttered as she swam into the cavern.

"I'm surprised you can show your face," Leilani commented as she passed.

"I was with them first," Velenka said.

"As their prisoner," the spinner retorted.

Gray slapped his tail against the cavern wall before everyone got to arguing. "Velenka, why are you here?"

The mako became a bit nervous, which was odd. It wasn't like her. "I, umm, I would like . . . to join your forces as a shiver shark so I can try out for the ghostfins."

"Whaaaaat?" Barkley almost shouted.

"I, for one, looove this idea," said Striiker.

Barkley glared at him.

"You have to admit she's gifted at being sneaky," the great white said.

"Doesn't matter," Shear put in. "Enemies can be gifted but they are still enemies."

"Thank you, Shear!" Barkley exclaimed.

"Why do you want to join?" Gray asked.

"Because he saved my life," Velenka said, pointing a fin at Barkley.

"You cannot be serious!" his friend blurted. "No, no, no!"

"Now that's interesting," Striiker quipped. "You kinda left that part out."

Barkley had glossed over what Velenka had been doing when the frilled shark attacked. He had told Gray about Snork's duel with the beast, which was incredible, but he'd said nothing about what happened with Velenka other than she got away in the confusion.

Certainly not that he had saved her life.

Velenka moved in front of Gray and gestured again at Barkley. "He saved my life and so I owe him. I can't go through life owing him."

"I didn't save you!" Barkley whined.

She nodded. "Yes, you did."

Barkley shook his head. "It wasn't on purpose."

"It kind of was," Leilani said.

He looked at the spinner. "Whose side are you on?

Velenka stared at Barkley with her big black eyes. "You hate me and yet your split-second reaction was to save me. It's . . . fascinating. And I can't have that hanging over my head."

"Graaay," Barkley said. "You're being very quiet and I don't like that. You're not considering this, are you? Come on."

Velenka flicked her fins. "I know things that would be useful," she said. "I was around Hokuu more than anyone. I can help stop him. That's very much in my interests as he's trying to send me to the Sparkle Blue."

Gray looked at Barkley and his friend sighed. He already knew.

"Fine," Barkley told Velenka. "But don't expect me to take it easy on you."

Takiza said, "I have some excellent techniques you can use to make sure she remains obedient, if you wish."

"I do wish," Barkley answered.

Gray slashed his tail through the water. "Okay, Velenka. But if there's even a hint that you're playing some sort of game, I will send Shear for you. There will be no excuses when he finds you. Understood?"

Velenka clicked her mouth shut and nodded.

Gray looked around the cavern, particularly at Velenka and Tydal. "It looks like we're not done fighting for peace, which I know is an odd thing to say. But war sometimes forces fins and dwellers who never had anything in common to become allies. We have to join together and figure out a way to beat the jurassics and whatever allies they manage to call. It won't be easy, so let's get to work."

And with that, they did.

play the game!

Sharpen your shark senses with:

- 8 challenging levels that put your skills to the ultimate test: hunt droves of slippery tuna and lightning-fast lobsters, fight killer crabs and hostile intruders, test your underwater navigation and swim speed, battle the rival sharks of Razor Shiver, and much more!
- Control options: joystick or tilt-to-swim
- Play as Gray or his best friend Barkley
- Hundreds of hidden objects and treasure
- Game Center leaderboards to challenge friends and outrank the world
- Updates on all the latest Shark Wars news and events
- The ultimate guide to the book series' main characters and shark clans

Download the FREE Shark Wars App at SharkWarsSeries.com

Acknowledgments

First I'd like to thank Ben Schrank, president and publisher of Razorbill, who took a huge chance by letting a first-time author write this book series.

Also in the Penguin family, thanks to Emily Romero, Erin Dempsey, Scottie Bowditch, Courtney Wood, Lisa Kelly, Anna Jarzab, Mia Garcia, Tarah Theoret, Shanta Newlin, Bernadette Cruz, and everyone else from marketing, publicity, and sales. My hardworking design and production team: Vivian Kirklin in managing editorial, Kristin Smith in design, and Amy White in production. And special thanks to Laura Arnold, my fantastic editor and fin-tastic conspirator on all things Shark Wars.

I'd also like to thank Wil Monte and his talented crew at Millipede Creative Development, led by Jason Rawlings, for creating the Shark Wars game. I hope to one day meet you lot in Melbourne for a pint. Thanks to illustrator Martin Ansin for the Shark Wars covers and endpapers, which look better than I could have ever imagined; and of course my agent Ken Wright at Writers House for all his hard work.

To my good friend Jim Krieg, who has done so much that I can never repay him, although I will certainly try. And finally to my family and friends who were so supportive through the years. Best wishes to you all.

EJ ALTBACKER is a screenwriter who has worked on television shows including *Green Lantern: The Animated Series*, *Ben 10*, *Mucha Lucha*, and *Spider-Man*. He lives in Hermosa Beach, California.

Visit **www.SharkWarsSeries.com** to learn more and to play the Shark Wars game!